Sweet Melodies

Sweet Melodies

A SINGER ROMANCE

WAFIYAH BASHA

Sweet Melodies

Two bands. One album to make. And trying not to fall in love.

My schedules are too tight, my days are a little too suffocating, but I never thought of complaining. After all, my dream had come true. I was the lead singer of the famous girl band in the world, *Celestials*. Things were going exactly how I envisioned it when I was 12. But what was not part of the plan was Callen Cox. He asked me to help him make an album with his band and I couldn't bring myself to say no. I found ways to help them in the music industry. I also found ways to fall head over heels in love with him. They say never mix business and love together. But why do I want us to be more than lingering touches and hidden feelings?

Ever since I held a guitar in my hand, I visioned. I would be standing on a stage, with my best friends playing their instruments in front of the thousands of adoring fans. That's all I ever wanted. To succeed in life. Aria helped my band and me with that vision of us. She helped us get a label, make an album, and make us the opening act of her tour. But the crowd didn't feel that appealing if she wasn't there, cheering for us. I started paying more attention to her than a friend and a business partner should. At the end of the day, whatever were the consequences, I wasn't afraid to have it. All I needed was her, my angel with me.

Author's note

Dear reader,

Thank you so much for picking up Sweet Melodies and even thinking of giving it a chance. This book will always be the most special one for me because this is my debut novel, my mark on this big world. The hard work that went into this making this is the product you hold in your hand right now. To follow my passion and dream and doing what I love is everything I have ever wanted.

Aria and Callen are even though my very first characters you read, it's not the last. Now, I know how amazing it feels writing for the world and I will publish more books for my readers.

I hope you enjoy this book. Cry when I cried and laughed when I laughed because I'm telling you, it's going to be a rollercoaster.

Happy reading!

Love,
Wafiyah

Playlist

"…Ready For It?"- Taylor Swift
"California Dreamin'"- The Beach Boys
"Eyes Off You"- PRETTYMUCH
"Come back…Be Here"- Taylor Swift
"this is me trying"- Taylor Swift
"Paradise"- Chase Atlantic
"Unsaid Emily"- Song by Julie and the Phantoms Cast
"Running Up That Hill (A Deal With God)"- Kate
Bush
"Angel Baby"- Troye Sivan
"Style"- Taylor Swift
"Secrets"- PLVTINUM, NEFFEX
"Softcore"- The Neighbourhood

To every person who wants to do what they are passionate about. You create your own stage. The audience is waiting for you.

The melodies are played
For you are the one who my heart sings for
Never would I sleep
Because it's you who I taint my dreams with
You are one in a million
The epitome of my love
Your hand is what I hold
As I lead you to the light
Fear not, my angel
You will be happy again
You will smile again
You will learn how to love again
Till then, I will love you. Silently.

Chapter 1

CALLEN

"I am sorry to tell you this, but… you're fired." I stare at Mr. Jackson like a sleepless owl.

"Excuse me?"

"You're fired." He repeats again with an ease of a thousand waterfalls. And I have a thousand fragile mirrors underneath those waterfalls, shattering at the force.

"But why?" I could already imagine the disappointment on my band mates faces.

This question catches Mr. Jackson off guard. He stumbles over words.

"Because the bar is facing a loss. We can't pay you anymore."

"You never paid us." I am exasperated. We literally played for free at his bar.

"We didn't? Oh well, that is awkward."

"Can you at least tell me what our band did wrong?" I was a person who always believed in improving from your mistakes. How else would you get better if you keep repeating the same idiocy over and over again?

"Your music isn't fresh anymore. The tunes are boring and frankly to tell you, the lyrics have no head or tail, it's just a mindless twitching body." Mr. Jackson ends with an apologetic tone.

Oh, that was quite frank.

I would have asked Mr. Jackson for a week to come with a new song, a fresh song that too. But it was promising that the river would stop flowing all of a sudden.

Tragedy hit Corruption, destabilizing all our members. The dreadful singer's block. We haven't written a good song for over three weeks. Not even when we put all our heads together. But we have had worse. Nothing beats The Block of 2020.

"I'm sorry, kiddo."

"It's okay, sir. Thank you so much for the opportunity." I raise from the stool bar and shake this hand over the counter.

"Good luck for the future." He waves goodbye and I nod at him with a smile.

Be optimistic, that's what my sister's encouragement poster said.

I head to my band, they are on the stage tuning the instruments.

"Guys, bad news." I announce.

"We are fired, aren't we?" Cade slumps his shoulder. This is the third time we have been fired in a year.

"Sorry." I shrug, pursing my lips.

Andrew curses quietly. We were going through training with Andrew to make him curse less and more silently.

Bad words are for your mouth not the public's ear. That's what Cade, who thought that we had to fix Andrew's foul mouth before we get famous, used to coo at Andrew like he is a monkey learning how to peel a banana.

"That Jackson, what a motherloader." Andrew snarls at the direction of the bar owner, serving definitely not tea. Another thing we taught him in his cursing lesson, substitution of words to the fewer offensives ones.

"Hey, what's up?" Edwin asks as he climbs the stage.

"Red cross." Cade answers and Edwin's face deflate.

"This job too? We were making these idiots hear us for free."

"I know. But we really can't do anything. Wherever we go, we have the same complaint. Not fresh and not catchy."

"Old Marco Jackson knows nothing about music, Callen." Cade offers. Our band has been facing difficulty that's for sure but this is the flat before the downfall and the downfall is not going to be good.

"So what should we do now? Play a last gig here?"

"Hell no. We aren't going to give that ducker another show of ours. Let's get out of here." Andrew suggested and we agreed.

"Actually, we might be able to go somewhere. Olivia has extra tickets to some concert. She asked me if we wanted to go but I told her we couldn't make it because we had this gig today. But apparently we don't have it anymore." Cade says. "If you want, I can call her and ask if they are still available."

Andrew threw one of his drumsticks on Cade. "Do it now, you asshole."

"Repeat that again." Cade challenges Andrew.

"Applehole?" He replies slowly and gets an approving nod from Cade.

Cade dials Olivia's number and she picks up the call in the second ring. Now, that's called love.

"Hey, baby. I have a small question. Do you still have the tickets for the concert you told me about?"

Whatever Olivia answers, does not fall to our earshot but Cade's smile ensures that she hasn't given or sold the tickets yet.

4

"Okay, we will meet you in an hour. Love you." He disconnects the call.

"She still has those tickets." Cade confirms our guess.

"Which concert is it?" Edwin asks.

"I forgot to get that detail."

"Cade." We three shout.

"Concert is a concert. It's better than sitting in a dingy bar or getting fired. Olivia is doing you all a favor by taking you with her so shut your yaps and be grateful."

"Yeah, whatever." Andrew starts packing his drums and we follow the suit with our instruments too.

I had no idea I would be getting fired this evening, neither did I know I would be going to a pure nameless concert. If our luck is better, it is most probably DJ Khaled and his anotha one's.

Olivia is already on her seats till we reach there, tethering through the crowd. Her auburn hair shines in the light that one girl from behind row shines to get through the darkness.

"Hey guys!" She waves excitedly at us. We all wave back as we take our seats and Cade kisses her as a form of greeting.

"Who are the Celestials?" I ask peeking forward.

Olivia's mouth drops open as if I asked an illegal question to her.

"You don't know who the Celestials are?"

"That's the reason why I am asking."

"God. You really need to get out of your hip hop music bubble and listen to other bands too."

"Just say who they are."

"Celestials are the greatest girl band. They started their band 2 years ago and till date, they have top singles, many No.1 charting songs, 2 albums released and a BRIT award. Do you know how difficult it is to get a BRIT so early in your music career? Yeah, Celestials did that." She continues.

"Not only do they make the most amazing songs that even the aliens and all other space creatures' dance around the universe, they are such strong, open minded girls. They fight for the right thing and they stand by it, no matter what others think. They break all norms, they bend societal rules, and they honestly just rock." She shrugs like it was a known fact.

I and the guys listen to her description. She seemed more than a fan, more like a person who idolizes the band. "You really like them, don't you?"

"I fucking love them." Olivia says with all seriousness and nothing else.

Okay, how great can this band be?

Before I can ask that, a loud sound booms through the speakers. I turn my head to the huge jumbotron-like screen on the front of the stadium we are in. A cloud dissipates on the screen, eerie music playing as the crowd cheers.

The show is starting.

A cool mash up of what I think is of their songs plays and everyone goes crazy as a video of the girls comes on the screen alongside with the mash up.

The music builds and builds till it goes off with pyrotechnics blasting like firecrackers and pink, yellow and blue colors floating with them.

The crowd screams. Literally screams as the band comes on stage.

"How is everyone doing tonight?" A girl says into the mic and a roar of happy screams is the response she gets.

"Excited, huh? Obviously, you all are. Celestials are going to grace you." She throws her hair behind her shoulder. She knows what she is.

6

I want a crowd like this for my band's concert. So exhilarated and responsive.

"As you all know, this is an out of schedule show we just thought of having and let me just say to you, we have many fan favorite songs." She teases the feverish crowd.

"But before we start, I would like you to thank the person who suggested this idea, our very own Aria." She gladly presents another girl dressed in black and golden costume.

People cheer as the camera for the jumbotron pans on the girl, Aria's face.

Aria's eyebrows rise at the cheers of the crowds. She is smiling.

"Well, thank you, Lexa. We indeed have kept this concert for our amazing fans. So to all Celestial beings that are rocking in the O2, sing with us." The tune starts playing and she pumps her hand in the air to the beat.

"*Are you ready for it?*"

Olivia reaches over Cade to me, "Be prepared to have your life changed. Nothing is the same after listening to Celestials."

"Oh. My. God." Andrew enunciates his words as the stadium lights come on.

Same brother, same. Celestials are amazing. Freaking amazing. Their songs made me dance and sing with them even if it's the first time I heard them.

"So?" Olivia asks with a cheeky smile on her face. She knew she made us their fan. Even Andrew is into them.

"They are mind-blowing." Edwin shakes his head like he can't believe it. "Breathtaking performance, stunning

7

voices and the choreography, are you kidding me? They were sensational."

She fists the air, "Yes! I made you Celestial beings."

"Are *Celestial being*s their fandom name?" Cade asks, spelling it out. The fandom's name sounded divine. Just like them.

"Is Aria their leader or something? She stood out within the four." Edwin asks.

"She isn't the leader." Olivia scrunches her nose. "But she is the one who assembled the band and signed most of their deals. If you want to talk about the band, you should talk to her. She takes care of everything. Not like a leader or manager, more like a Mama bird. She really loves her group."

"She is hot though." Edwin comments.

"The hottest." Olivia agrees.

"So Callen, what are your thoughts?" She asks me slyly. Everyone turns to listen to my answer.

"I think I am going to start listening to their songs." I admit with a smile.

Chapter 2

ARIA

I live for this.

The scream of the fans, the happy screams only for *you*. Their lives changed because of *you*. Their happiness blooms for something *you* do. This is what dreams are made of. And I am living it.

My dream of making myself useful has always been my motivation to stand on stage and do what I love the most. When I do this, I know. This is life. An unexpected turn down the road, but a wonderful destination all the same.

"Great job everyone! Amazing show." Lexa cheers, our own personal cheerleader. And everyone hollers at her compliment.

"You were on fire." Zeenat hip bumps me and I laugh.

"I think I am on fire. This costume is inflammable with sweat and heat."

"It's fash-hunnn." She gives me a playful shrug as she walks past on the way to the locker room. As I follow her, I can only shake my head.

We open the door and pause as we see Ver hunched over the couch.

"Ver, are you okay?" I rush toward her.

"Period cramps." She groans, clutching her abdomen. Her forehead shines with sweat as she turns to her back, completely pale.

"Oh sweetie, when did it start?" I ask, pushing her hair off her sticky forehead. Zeenat hands me a towel, kneeling beside the couch and I pat Ver.

"During the performance. When we took a water break while tuning, I felt it. Oh god." Her face pinches in pain. Another attack of cramps.

"You should have told us something." Zeenat says.

"I know but I knew you guys wouldn't proceed with the choreography if I told you I am on my periods. We worked hard for this show."

"Yeah, we work hard for every performance but you know that health comes first. Our fans are not going to ask for a refund if we don't dance." My voice rises a little in the end. This was stupidity. Who dances the hell out of our upbeat songs when they just got their periods?

Zeenat swipes her hand on my knee, her eyes pleading for me to cool down.

I sigh.

"Just tell us next time. Nothing matters to us more than us ourselves. Okay?" I tell to Ver and she nods.

I pick my phone and call our tour manager, Niya.

"Hello there, superstar." She answered the call with. "The show was amazing by the way. I really liked it when you did the triple cartwheel."

I laugh. "Thank you. That was quite a stunt. Listen Niya, we need your help."

I look at Ver's tired body and my heart fills with worry.

"Sure, go ahead. Booze to celebrate a successful show?"

"Ugh, no. I need sanitary pads, loose clothes and something sweet. And a car back to our hotel."

"Okay, the monthly drill. Got it." She disconnects the phone. It's been two years since we became famous, third year going strong. Ver has had her periods 24 times when we travelled and I know what she wants every time. The monthly drill, as Niya quotes. Clothes that don't suffocate her body, food because a girl gotta eat and sweet items. She craves the hell out of sweets.

"Get her out of her clothes and let her take a shower. It is safe to say we all are sweaty messes."

Zeenat gives me a salute. She helps Ver in the bathroom and I get outside to fetch Lexa.

There is no sign of her as I search the brick wallpapered hallways.

I finally find her making out with a boy which I am pretty sure was a part of sound systems.

I clear my throat and they break apart. She sneers at me and I smirk.

"Alexa Sangria, mind coming?" I say innocently.

"Yeah, you can take her. We were not doing anything important anyways." The boy waves off, blushing.

She turns to him with wide eyes. Okay, he was about to get punched by her manicured hands.

"Lex?"

She squares her jaw. "Coming."

As we turn the corner to our room, she raises her middle finger to the boy. Classic Lexa.

""I appreciate you getting me off that ass, but why the cock block?"

"Code Red. Ver is exhausted. Car will be here soon. By the way, should I put you on a leash or GPS tracker so you don't go off sucking boys' faces?"

"Hardy har har." She scrunches her nose at me, teasingly. "I am an independent grown woman."

"You're not even legal to drink yet." I point it out.

11

"Seriously, who even keeps 21 as the drinking age? It is dumb if you ask me."

"The government decides it. It's called the law."

"Well, fuck the law."

"Be careful before someone listens to you and you are airing in the news tomorrow morning because of your political comment."

"Truth is truth." She shrugs. That is one of our mottoes. We don't sugarcoat the truth or let it dissolve within the lies, we stand for it.

But the legal age to drink is not a national problem.

"Atta girl." I pat her back. Zeenat is on the phone, talking to someone and I hear the shower run.

Everyone is here and safe. Good.

My phone pings with a message, Niya just texted.

Tour manager Niya*: The car is waiting outside for you and the girls. I have set up everything in your room, sweet and fluffy blankets. Tell Ver to take care of herself. Love you girls!*

True gem for us. I reply to her back with hearts.

Ver comes out of the washroom, dressed in loose clothing.

"Are we ready to go?" I ask them and they nod.

We take our bags and Lexa takes her kitten, Benjamin Buttons. Yes, a very creative name.

She is Taylor Swift when she names her pets.

I see Ver struggle to keep a straight posture so I help her out. I hold her bag in one hand and sling her long arm over my shoulder.

"Thanks, A."

"Mention not." I support her. Periods are truly a huge pain in the ass. Back too.

"I miss Cash." She mumbles, sadly.

Cash, full name, Cashmere is a rapper and her boyfriend. They were together for a long, long time It was

12

a high school romance and lasted till now. Bravos and kudos to them.

Cash was actually a good guy. There are many breeds of men like how there are substantially different breeds of monkeys.

There were assholes, raised good, misogynist, playboys, stone cold, possessive and The One.

The One is the category Cash belonged to. Those oddly genetically engineered men just made for their other half.

Cash and Ver fit like pieces in a puzzle. A 500 pieces of a puzzle with 250 pieces Ver and 250 pieces Cash. They were complex and big personalities. But somehow they still fit together.

"I know, sweetie. You can meet him tomorrow."

We were traveling back to home tomorrow.

"I hope so." She lulls her head on my shoulder. "Aria?"

"Yes."

"Promise me we won't be touring and sudden concerts for at least 6 months. I really want to spend some time with Cash."

I was overworking my band, I got the feeling.

"I promise. But I hope you both do something good during this 6 month tour break."

"Really?" She smiles. "Like what?"

"Oh, I don't know. But I would be happy to become an aunt."

"Let him propose to me first. Babies are a later topic." She answers, laughing.

I open the car door for her and she scoots into the car seat. I follow the same, closing the door.

The girls are exhausted. Even Benjamin Buttons can keep his eyes barely open, he cuddles with Lexa. Zeenat dozes off and Ver lays her head on my lap, wrapped in a blanket. It was a good 20 minutes ride to the hotel we were staying at so I took out my iPad and notebook to work on my band's schedule.

Chapter 3

CALLEN

Everyone had a place for them to kick back and relax. Some had their house. Some had home. I was the lucky one. I got a home.

I knock at the door, gathering my jacket around me tightly.

The door swings open to my sister's grinning face. "Coxo!"

"Hey Missy." I step in, shrugging my jacket off. We had a heater in our home and it was already warm inside.

"Who is at the door, Missy?" I hear Mom calling out from the kitchen, I guess.

"Your prodigal son has returned, mother." She answers, closing the door. "Who hasn't had his big break yet and still comes to meet his parents early on a Saturday morning."

"I missed you, Missy." "

"What is that supposed to do to me? Does your missing have a monetary value? Can I use it for my future? No, right? So you know where to shove it."

My 19 year old sister, Missy, who hates feelings.

Mom comes to the living room. Her eyes light up seeing me. I remember, this is what I live for. I love my family and even if their eyes light up a little brighter, even if their smiles last a little longer, I would do anything for it.

Even by becoming successful and helping them out from this home to a better place. Where they can make their home, a happier one.

"Cally. How are you, baby?" She extends her arm and I gladly seek refuge in them.

"Hi, Mum."

"Are you coming to your grandpa's party? He would love it."

"Yes, mum. I will be there."

"Good. Now that you came over, there are pancakes and your favorite bacon in the kitchen, help yourself. You have become so thin."

Before I could ease her worries, Missy speaks up, pushing past me.

"I think he looks fine. Actually, he has gotten fatter."

"Strike two. Insult me again and see what I do to you."

"Bring it on. I have been working out for the past 3 months. Let's see who kicks whose ass." She challenges me.

"I am going to fetch your father." Mom tells us. "Just don't kill each other." She gives a pointed look before leaving upstairs.

"So, have you become a famous singer yet?"

"At least I don't sit at home half of the day."

"That's not true. Half day at college, half day partying. You know the drill. Oh wait, you don't. Because you were busy playing with your dork band." She cackles at her joke.

I smirk. I have absolute ammunition to bring her down.

I casually stroll to get a plate and fill it up with food. I sit on the dining table elegantly and Missy watches my

15

move like a hawk. Stuffing the softest pancakes into my mouth with my right hand, I pull my phone out of the pocket with the left one. On Whatsapp, I have the pictures that Olivia sent me. I forward it to Missy.

"Hey, check out the pictures I sent you." I say nonchalantly.

"Okay." She narrows her eyes at me and reaches for her phone over the counter.

She unlocks the phone, switching her gaze between me and her phone.

She plays the first video and I can't stop grinning. She is going to be so mad.

Celestials's *Brand Me Now* played with Oliva singing with them. I have seen that video before. The video focuses on the stage, a close up on the band before it panned on me and my friends.

"Holy hell." She gasps.

I don't say anything. Letting her grasp her own reality.

"You went to a Celestials concert?" She basically shouts it out.

"Yes, I did." I chuckle at her shocked face.

"Tell me you're joking."

"The photographic proof is right there." I shrug at her disbelief.

She stares at the video once again and lets out a frustrated scream. "Not fair, I love them so much. You most probably didn't even hear their name."

"That is so not true." I act highly offended. Yeah, maybe I didn't know who they were before their concert. But better late than never right?

"Why are you screaming?" Dad asks Missy as he enters the kitchen.

"Callen went to a Celestials concert!" She rats me out with her pointed witchy finger.

"Oh cool. How was it?" He turns his attention to me.

"You know who the Celestials are?" I ask, confused. Since when do parents know the latest bands?

"Those girls are amazing singers. Ver is my favorite. So is Zeenat." He rubs his chin like I asked whether what is more important, oxygen or oxygen. "I don't know, both of them are stunning."

"What about Aria?" I casually dropped it. It would be bashful to admit that I had the tiniest crush on her.

"Aria? She is everyone's favorite, kid. Even mine."

"Who is your favorite?" Mom asks as she follows him in.

"Dad likes a girl band." I snitch out to Mom. She glares at my Dad and I pop a piece of bacon in my mouth. I loved getting Dad into harmless trouble. It was fun how he defends himself against a force like Mom.

"Ahhaa, you like girl bands nowadays." She interrogates, putting her hands on her hips.

"Honey, he is joking, you know that." Dad covers up.

"No, Mom. You know I never joke like Missy. He actually likes them." I nod earnestly, turning towards Dad. "What were you telling, Dad? Something that Ver and Lexa are amazing at. Is that right, Dad? Were those your words?" I query, grinning at his red face.

"Son of a bitch." He curses lowly. A curse not low enough to surpass a mother's ears.

"Excuse me?" Mom widens her eyes at him.

"No, baby. I didn't say anything."

Mom leaves the kitchen and Dad follows her, begging sorry profusely.

"You're an ass, you know that." Missy takes a seat on the other side of the table. "But steak dinner tonight."

We high five. Dad always took us somewhere fancy whenever Mom was pissed with him. There were countless times we lit up fights between them so we could get fancy food. But all of them were harmless fights.

Missy and I catch each other up on our lives as we have breakfast while our Dad suffers in the clutches of marriage.

"Wait seriously?"

17

I nod grimly. "That's what the guys are suggesting. We can't do our daily small gigs. It's been 4 years since the band was formed and we still haven't gotten out into the world. It's a really painful process."

The guys have been very upset over our last job. We needed the money and the tips we got in the bar sufficed us, until now.

"So you are going to start sending demos to the records, hoping you get in somehow?"

"Somehow." I release a tired sigh.

"Didn't you tell me that Aria from Celestials is in charge of her band?"

"Yeah, that's what Olivia told me."

"Why don't you ask her then?"

"Ask her what?"

"Ask Aria if she and her band is up for a collab." She says like why the hell the idea not came in my mind before.

"If Corruption's name is only shown in their music video, people will know who you are and they will start listening to your songs. Just imagine what would happen if you guys collaborated with Celestials, that's it, written in the history books."

"You can't be serious."

"I am. Celestials can be your big break. Those girls are huge around the world. They are like the female version of One Direction. Even if a quarter of their fans listen to your band, you are set for life. And no record company will rest until they sign Corruption."

"Really?"

"Yes, moron. This could be a solid plan."

Maybe. Aria is the part of the biggest girl band. Why would she collab with a band that no one has heard of except our mothers? But there could be a chance where she thinks we are worthy enough to even feature in their video. Then we could have a meteoric success.

It wouldn't hurt to try, would it?

18

Chapter 4

ARIA

"Take a break, Ari." Zeenat says, following her words with a yawn. She leaned over our home recording studio's doorframe with her robe and coffee on.

I stubbornly shake my head. I have been up since 5am, trying to be productive and write songs. The darn brain isn't working. I strum the guitar, figuring out a tune which could be our next song. I was fine till yesterday evening but the awful writer's block is attacking me this morning.

"Why do you do so much?"

"That is a bit insulting." I answer with a smile.

"Hey, you know what I mean. You work too hard. We all deserve a day off. You should take at least an hour off because I know you will get mad otherwise."

"You do realize that if we all didn't work so hard, we wouldn't be where we are right now." I point it out to her with my pencil. "You would be doing a degree and not even know what to major in. Ver would have taken over her family's oil company even though she doesn't know shit about it. And Lexa would have been in the adult filming business."

Zeenat laughs. "Lexa fits that part well, doesn't she?"

"Obviously she does. She is sexy and she knows it." I catch a tune and proceed on with it. Quickly, I press the record button on my phone. I documented all my sessions. We never know when one lyric or melody on the piano might resonate with you.

As it starts getting good, I lose it. "Fuck." I mutter, hanging my head low in defeat.

"It's fine, Ari. That riff was really good. Why don't you take a break and then we all will work on that." Zeenat consoles me.

But I hear the same sentence over and over in my head. *We need more! We need more! We need more!*

Maybe a peaceful and fun session with the girls is maybe something I needed. Back when we were just geeks in freshman year of high school, Ver made donuts and her world class chocolate muffins for our writing session. We gossiped, laughed and wrote songs. We didn't have any pressure.

We were a band for fun and sometimes we played at our school dances and birthday parties.

Then we started playing at Marco's bar for a year. That's where we gained our confidence to face the real world.

The effort we put in for reaching the level we are in right now is all because of our collective hard work and countless sleepless nights. We worked our ass off.

But when you dream for something, you forget that it comes with its own consequences. There is always a pressure from the world to have more from you. It was like an endless run on the marathon and never reaching the finishing line.

"Yes, we will do that. Till you guys get ready and wake up completely, I will go on a run."

20

Running is my option to everything. Feeling tired? Run. Feeling sick? Run. Feel like your brain is about to burst with annoyance and self-deprivation? Simple, *run*.

"Aria." Zeenat scolds but I kiss her cheek and gather my ear buds and phone.

"I need this, sweetie." I shrug like there is no other option for me. "Be ready and awake till I come. Make sure that others are too."

They are wake up but are not awake till they have their coffees.

She salutes.

Zeenat was the oldest one in the group. Three months older than me. Ver was a month younger than me and Lexa was still 20 years old. It is funny to see her as the only 20 in the group of 21's.

Zeenat was an old friend. She has visited home since I was a kid. She became my elder sister when mine was taken away. She worried and took care of me when I was working late. Others also work but I go overboard. She was always there to pull me down a notch to the right amount of obsessiveness.

Zeenat was associated with someone I try to avoid thinking of. The glimpses float like a teasing angel in my mind and I curse internally. *Not now.*

This directly dims my mood. Despair on more despair.

I am out of the gate and into the streets, hoping that paparazzi do not catch me in the mood I am in right now.

I quickly plug my ear buds in before I drift away.

Chase Atlantic plays and I release a breath of relief. Their music is what I need to keep every single problem at bay.

I jog, taking in the surroundings. The sun was just rising. The sky resembles a blue cotton candy that my dad bought for me in the Summer Fair when I was 8. People are barely out on the street. I like to think of them still curled up in their blankets with their alarms snoozed for the next 3 hours before getting late to work. They were humans after all, not machines.

I come across a small park which I think I have seen before on my car rides to the studios. There is a small fountain in the middle and it's cute.

I rest on the slab, catching my breath. The cool morning breeze with tiny drops of water hits my sweaty back. I close my eyes, taking in the silence.

That doesn't last not very long as someone calls me.

I check the caller ID before taking it.

"Good morning, Ms. Bastian."

"Morning, Kate. How are you?"

"I am good, miss. Let's go over your morning schedule?"

"Fire away."

And she does fire away.

Kate was our personal assistant. The sweetest and most obedient soul ever. She is punctual which is necessary when you are in a band that needs to be on shows and places on time.

She is attentive and the most perfect assistant I can ask for. Every morning at 6am, she calls me to go through my schedule. Honestly, I would have done this on my own but there is so much my tired brain can take.

"What is at 11:30 again?" I ask.

"Mr. Suxxen. He is the new artist manager."

"I liked Calisto." I grumble. I liked him unless he thought that he should quit his job, take his wife and travel the world. Good for his wife, I suppose. Us? Simply put, not very much.

"Mr. Suxxen sounds good too. Just try okay? If you don't like him as your artist manager, then we will look for another one. Just try." Kate reasons.

"Okay." I promise. "Anything else for this eventful morning?"

"Yeah, one last doubt. There is this guy who keeps calling to book an appointment with you. What should I do?"

"Really? Are you sure he is not a creep or something?"

"Well, he sounds sane to me."

"What's his name?" I hear the rustling of papers.

"His name is. . .Callen" I rack my brain for that name. When you're a singer, you meet many people but Callen doesn't ring a bell.

"I don't know him."

"Do you want to meet him?"

"Sure, squeeze him in. But make sure he is legitimate."

It wouldn't hurt to see who it is, would it?

I drum the table with my fingertips.

"Are you scared?" Lexa observes. I bark out a laugh.

"Scared? Name one time have you seen me scared."

"Then what emotion has got you jittery, Ms. Fearless?"

"Curiosity." I answer, nodding earnestly.

"You're so full of yourself. You know that?" She flips her hair behind her shoulder. *Look who's talking.*

"I am enlightened, thank you very much."

The door opens and the latecomer greets us.

"Good morning, Ms. Bastian." He shakes my hand. A good firm business handshake is the first thing I notice but that doesn't deviate me from the fact that he is late.

"Afternoon actually. You are half an hour late."

"Technically it is still 11:59 so I was right about the greeting." He jokes.

Lexa sucks in a breath. I hate being called wrong. I glance at the clock. There were still 15 seconds to 12pm. My jaw ticks.

"Don't try to be smart with me, Mr. Suxxen." I say, my eyes holding a warning that won't be repeated again.

His face loses half of its color. "I am sorry, miss."

"Why don't you sit, Mr. Suxxen? By the way, my name is Lexa." She forwards her hand to him and he clings on it like a lifeboat.

"Nice to meet you, Lexa."

We sit down on the long conference table and get to business. He pitches his ideas and ways we can market ourselves even more.

"And obviously, you will have a tour this year." He marks one thing off his list.

"Actually, we won't be touring this year." I quickly speak up.

"What? Why?" Lexa whines. She loves to tour. Her favorite part was traveling.

Sorry Lex, I made a promise to Ver.

"Because we are going to work on a new album for the next few months. The shooting of music videos, promo and launching will keep us busy for this year. Next year, we will go on tour, don't worry." I direct this to Lexa but Suxxen finds it as an opportunity for him to speak up.

"I think it's better if you tour this year."

I ground my jaw together, turning to him. "And why would you think that?"

"To increase your sales."

"And albums don't increase sales?"

"I agree with her. Albums are always a huge hit for us." Lexa favors me.

"Tour is fixed. We know that you will sell out each show. The merchandise is another source of income too. Who gives us a guarantee that your album will be a hit?" He shamelessly asked.

I scoff to myself. What a wrong person to mess with Suxxy.

"Only if our last two albums were not just the most famous and best sold ones. Listen, Mr. Suxxen. We know what we do and we do it damn good. So when one song has sold triple of how much you make, you should know to shut your mouth and let the more, how do I say this? Experienced and better ones take the lead."

If he was paled out before, he is fucking white paper now.

Lexa throws me a '*what the hell*' look but I ignore it.

"Never, never, question our hard work and integrity. We worked our ass off in the last two albums and best believe we will go for the third one too. If you can't value us then I would like, *love*, for you to give your resignation letter to my assistant, Kate." I tilt my head to the side. "She is a pretty blonde in a red blouse."

Lexa tells him to drink water while we take a break.

"Why do you always have a stick up your ass?" She scolds.

"Stick is low class. I have a diamond crystal rod."

"You can do better than this, Aria. You are better than this."

"Have it ever crossed you that I don't want to?" I relax back on the chair, smiling.

"You are normally so friendly."

"So what?"

"So go easy on Mr. Suxxen. Sure he can have different views from the ones you established like the Royal Decree in your head but give him a chance."

"Go easy on me. I can listen to Adele's lyrics."

"Sure you can." She pats me encouragingly and red face Mr. Suxxen enters the room again. For the next one hour, we got through the meeting with many restraints from Lexa. Suxxen dialed his stupidity down so it wasn't that bad.

"Thank you for your time, Ms. Bastian and Lexa. It was an honor." Mr. Suxxen says, piling papers he came in with. He really did put a lot of thought into this meeting.

"Mr. Suxxen?"

"Yes, miss."

"Sign the contract on your way out." I release the sentence with difficulty. Sure, he was a bit annoying but his ideas were not half as bad and I really think he can fit with us in an imperfect way and bring things to table, good things.

"Really?" He asks with surprise and a wide set of eyes.

"Yes." I say, backtracking for the fun of it. "Unless obviously you don't want to?"

"No no, I want to." He covers up. "Thank you so much, Ms. Bastian. Thank you." He walks out of the room with a skip in his step.

"See, that wasn't that bad. You made the man happy." Lexa appreciates it.

"Yeah, whatever." I get up, dismissing her compliment.

Lexa and my phone start ringing at the same time, different tunes. We exchange a look before checking the caller ID. Mine said Ver while hers had our house landline number calling her.

This can't be good.

I answer the call with my heart beating in my throat.

Chapter 5

CALLEN

The sole of my shoe tapped against the white marbled tiled floor, anxiously. They were still in the conference room.

Agreeably I was here early. 2 hours early.

But I couldn't help it. Aria's assistant, Kate, agreed to get me an appointment with her. It's been two weeks since Missy gave me the push I needed and it took another two weeks to get the appointment.

I thought that it would take more time keeping in mind how famous Aria's band is but Kate told me that her boss has agreed to see me today. The day my grandpa turns 80. I was dressed up for two reasons: The meeting and grandpa's birthday.

A man, quite chubby, comes out of the conference room. He looks worked up and pale. He directly heads to the water cooler and grabs a plastic cup. Kate looks at him and a pity look comes across her expression.

What is happening in that conference room?

"Is everything alright, Mr. Suxxen?" Kate asks.

The man, Mr. Suxxen, sighs. "What can go right?"

Kate chuckles lightly. "She can be a little uptight, sir. But she means well for her band, I promise."

"I guess she does." He agrees with her, nodding, his thick bush of hair moves with his agreement.

"Believe me, she does. So go in there and listen to her but don't cower away from your opinion because she likes her management members filled with confidence. If you listen to what I say then I guarantee you will have a two year contract by the time you exit that room."

Suxxen stares at her like he is trying to figure out what to do. Either stay or go running for the hills.

"Thank you, Miss Kate. You have been very helpful." He slaps his cheeks twice, readying himself for whatever lies on the other side of the door and charges inside. I half expected him to sing a war cry.

I drift back to Kate and she is already looking at me as if she knows what is going on in my mind. "She's not bad, you know."

"Seems like you have been up lifting her image a lot around here." I notice.

"That's because I know her very well. You won't find a loving, kind soul like her in this world." By saying this, she goes back to doing her work.

I sit quietly, repeating her sentence in my mind. *Loving, kind soul like her.*

Do they still make those?

I wait for one more hour, swiping TikTok videos on my phone in low volume. The door swings open and Mr. Suxxen comes into the reception, prancing like a pony.

"I got the job!" He squeals and high fives Kate with both of his hands. He signs the contract and I stare dumbfounded.

All this guy did was spend 2 hours with Aria, increase his blood pressure and get the job. I don't know which job but he got a job with Aria.

"I told you to listen to me." Kate gloats to the man and he doesn't seem to care that much, he is on cloud 9.

I start feeling nervous. What if my meeting doesn't go well? What if I am not flying onto the highest skies when I am out of that door?

The same door opens again and I see her.

Aria. In flesh and halo light.

She is wearing a red shirt and gray plaid pants. Everything about her screamed formal and business. She strides on her high heels, clinking as another girl who if I am not wrong was her other band mate, Lexa right behind her.

I catch her look as she wheezes past where I sit.

A scared one.

"Kate, cancel all our meetings for today." Lexa says with urgency to the receptionist.

"Is something wrong?" Kate's eyes dart between Aria and Lexa's face.

"It's an emergency. Just cancel all the meetings. We will coordinate on the phone later."

As soon as Aria speaks the clipped sentence out, she and Lexa dash to the elevator.

"Ms. Bastian, where are you going?" Kate calls to her but Aria takes the place by a storm and is dissipated into the fading thin air. Kate is left speechless.

"What was that about?" Suxxen asks, clueless.

"I have no idea." She shakes her head. "Are you done with signing?"

"Yeah, I am." He hands her the stack of paper and she files it.

Kate turns her attention to me as the man leaves. "As you saw and heard." She gestures apologetically towards the elevator.

I rise from the seat. My legs are stiff from sitting down way too long. "It's fine. Maybe it was an emergency."

"You are understanding. I hope all the other clients are the same as you when I call them and say that the meeting is canceled."

I smile a little. "You are doing good, Kate."

She thanks me and picks up the landline.

I walk out of the place and to my car. I was looking forward to this meeting but if things don't work your way, what can you do?

A part of me thought that they were playing hooky from work but the thought vanishes when I remember the look on Aria's face.

Her fear was readable. Something happened to her loved one, I think. She felt like she was wasting those tragic seconds.

All I wish is whatever happened would turn out to be okay.

I drove off to my grandpa's eight decade birthday party with a debating mind.

Chapter 6

ARIA

My heart is hammering in my chest.

I can't hear anything. I can't feel anything. I am running to the operating room that is playing with Zeenat's life in its mischievous hands.

The moment I heard about Zeenat's accident. It sucked me into the past. The events were repeating themselves. And I for once won't stand in the corner and be a bystander.

I skid across the floor and the nurse jumps at my entry.

"Aria!" Ver shouts as she spots me and throws herself with desperate arms on me.

"Where is she?"

"She's getting operated."

I pat Ver's back, silently asking her to move off me. I wasn't trying to be insensitive. I wanted to check on Zeenat first. After that, I will be distributing hugs and cookies around the hospital for all I care about.

The red bulb over the operation theater shone like a menace. An undeniable urge to push my way into the room and see Zeenat wrecked my body but I resisted.

She is getting operated on, I can't.

I sit back on the chair, defeated. My heart squeezes involuntarily. This was not how I imagined my afternoon to go. To be sitting in the crappy metal chair, waiting for my friend's operation to be done.

I replay the image I created in my head after Ver told me what happened.

Zeenat was working in the home studio, she came down to get something, slipping and falling down the stairs. She hit her head at the corner.

Lexa and I were at the meeting with Suxxen, Ver was having her yoga session in the nearby gym. With no one in the home, she bled on the cold floor.

The rest went as it goes. When Ver came back from her session, she found Zeenat. 911. Called us. We came rushing. Zeenat in the operation theater.

I swipe a sweaty palm over my face. I hated how this situation was so familiar. The only thing different now was that I am twenty one, not seventeen. Four years seems centuries ago yet somehow it felt like it was yesterday.

A pair of legs came in front of me.

"Hi, are you Aria?" They ask, and I lift my head to see who it is.

A man with a kind face looks down at me. not with pity, but with regard. He has a white coat around him. A doctor. "Yes."

"I guessed. Can you please tell me your full name please?" He asks, pen ready on the clipboard.

"Aria Ryanne Bastian."

"Well, it's nice to meet you, Aria Ryanne Bastian. You are Zeenat's emergency contact. I just wanted to make sure that it's really you."

"Will she be okay?" My voice breaks even when I don't want it to.

His face softens. "Yes, she will. She does have a deep cut, but luckily there is no damage to her brain. Most of the time, we are praying for a concussion and nothing serious."

"Thank you." I pause because I don't know his name.

"Cameron Cox."

"Thank you, Dr. Cox."

The doctor leaves, and I slum back into the chair and close my eyes. The same thing is cycling in my head.

I spent two hours in the hospital for emotional support. But after that, I couldn't take it anymore. The antiseptic smell and quick reflexes of the nurse and doctors greet a new victim. These walls held too many bad memories.

"I am going to check in with the office." I inform Lexa. Ver is sleeping on her shoulder.

"Okay. Take care. Get an hour of sleep if possible."

I don't want to leave them. But I can't breathe in this place. "Be careful. Give me a call if anything happens."

She nods and I turn to leave.

"Aria?" Lexa calls out.

"Hmm?"

"This shall pass too." Sadness coats her face. From her face, it was clear she knew how I was feeling.

Tears fill my eyes. "I know." I bite my lip, walking out of the waiting room.

I sit in the car. As I start the engine, I rack my brain for where to go right now.

The place, which is not my favorite, pops into my mind.

With Zeenat in the hospital, work looming, and no help from outside, that was the only place that drew me in.

Somewhere along the way, I sought peace and solace. Somewhere, the clock didn't tick and the world didn't rotate. Where the time was always the same, heavy and empty.

I started driving.

Two hours down the road and one pee break later, I feel a little better.

The dark road and even darker music are the perfect combination for the mood I am in right now.

Lexa messaged me half an hour ago that Zeenat has stabilized. Now, she was under observation and still unconscious.

Kate left me a voicemail on my schedule for tomorrow.

And I am on my way to visit my hometown at 7 in the evening.

There weren't many cars on the road. People preferred staying home on a Sunday while I went all over the place.

I squint my eyes as I spot something on the side of the road, far off.

As I get closer, I realize it's not something but someone.

There was a man—I could tell from his build—who had his head in the hood of the car, and I am pretty sure smoke was coming out of it.

It was dark, and he didn't seem to have any help getting off the road.

I knew better than to leave anyone on the side of the road without help.

I stop my car right next to his and honk to get his attention.

Chapter 7

CALLEN

A loud honk resonates through the empty road and I jump, banging my head on the hood at the sound of it.

I wince, rubbing the back of my head.

A black Mustang pulled up near my car burns its headlight into my grown to the darkness eyes. I squint trying to see the driver but couldn't make out the figure behind the wheel properly.

The car door opens, and a figure steps out. A girl with shoulder-length hair and curves

"Hi, do you have a problem with your car?" She sounds so sweet and kind that I almost melted into a puddle at that question.

"Yeah, kind of." I wince at the sight of the engine. It didn't look good. Not even in pitch dark.

"Do you mind if I check it out?" She points towards the hood of the car.

She walks towards me and I notice one thing quickly. She smells *good.*

Her nose scrunches as she sniffs the air.

"Smoke is not a good sign." She says to herself.

"Well, I am just happy that the car didn't blow up in flames." I joke, proceeding on to the most awkward laugh I ever voiced.

The girl stares at me like I am weird but then I hear a small chuckle pass her lips.

She *actually* found that funny? I expected her to ignore me or give a pity laugh.

That didn't sound like a pity laugh.

"Let me shine my torch on it." She pulls her phone out of the pocket. Her screen lights up and I manage to take a peek at the time.

6:57pm. I was supposed to be at my grandpa's party 2 hours ago, helping them set up.

As soon as I left the canceled meeting at KVN Labels, I headed back to my place for a sad nap and then hopped into my car to drive to the birthday party.

Half way down the grainy road, my car started acting up. It whirred, it groaned and stopped. Somehow no one had plans to come to the suburbs this Sunday so there were no cars on the road and with waiting duration to fossilize.

My phone's battery died long back because I was watching TikToks in the waiting room and it didn't cross my useless brain even once to charge it before leaving the home.

This girl, whoever she is, is a really good smelling angel to me.

She shines her torch from the phone on the engine. There's a huge mess on the spot she shone on. It's leaking and doing something weird. I can't even intercept it.

"Whoa, that definitely doesn't look good." I turn, say and stop. My mouth hangs open. From the light illuminated, it created a halo effect on the girl's face.

On goddamn Aria's face.

"I know, it's busted." She agreed with me and I try to think of what I just said.

"Where do you keep your tools?" She asks, looking directly at me.

I gulp the tingly sensation in my throat and my hands clam up.

"In the trunk." I manage to sputter it out.

"Okay." She goes back and I start hyperventilating.

Aria. Aria was right in front of me. She shone her touch on my car's busted engine. She spoke to me. She is right now opening my car's trunk, talking about my tool box. Well, not mine exactly but my brother's. But who cares about the ownership? He is a doctor and can get whatever he wants with his paycheck.

Aria is back to the front. I step out of her way so I don't interrupt whatever she is doing. I control my breathing so she doesn't hear me losing it in the dead silence of the night.

"Can you hold up the phone for me?"

"Ye uh. I mean, yeah sure." I take the phone she is holding out and her fingers brush. *Oh fuck.*

She takes some tools I don't know the names of and starts working on the engine.

When the paranoia calms down, I start taking notice of her work. She skillfully fixes like she knows what she is doing.

"Where did you learn how to do this from?" I ask, amazed.

I always thought that great singers and bands like hers were born with playing instruments, obviously not mechanical tools.

"My dad taught me more than changing tires."

"Sounds like a wise guy." I observe.

"The best, if you ask me. This world is divided into two halves. A ridden male and a repressed female The males have glowing opportunities fed to them like silver spoons from the day they are born. Where girls are buried in the ground before they even have a chance to live. Their tombstones have their roles and they have to perform them

37

no matter what. A good, obedient wife, a great mother, an unemployed red wine drinker, a pushover, and a sex object. People in this world treat women like a step on the stairs or a rug on the ladder. And we live in the 21st century." She scoffs at herself. "But my dad must have kept a mindset of the 22nd century because he made sure that I and my sister knew everything and feared nothing. He should be a role model for all men out there. Astronauts and pilots can go to hell when you aren't a good human being."

"Men irritate you?" I quirk my eyebrows.

"The irritating ones do." She says. "In my career, we tend to be objectified a lot. And called names which make me think who even made those words. Everyone feels like it's their right to have a say in our lives."

"How do you deal with it?"

"You'll never be able to deal with it, you know. You just push it away, put it in the rearview mirror, and try not to look. Just try not to think." A faraway look comes on her face, it looks like she is alone in an empty place. All alone.

"Sounds like healthy advice." I comment.

She pulls out her trance and laughs. A small laugh but still a laugh.

"Well, it keeps the demon at bay." She wipes her hands off in the pants and I try to guess how much they cost.

"I did fix it but I don't think it can go that far and by seeing that you are stranded in the middle of the road, you most probably are planning to travel for a long distance. So it's better if you call a tow truck." She advises and I nod at her every word. Calling a tow truck and going back home sounds like a good plan.

"Oh shit." I curse as realization dawns on me.

"What happened?" Aria questions.

"My phone died." I break it to her, racking my head for what I should do.

"Well, RIP to it." She remarks. "Where were you planning to go anyways?"

I might have thrown a startled look because she backtracks. "If you don't mind me asking."

"My grandpa's birthday."

"How old?"

"80." I wince as I say it. With an age like his, it might well have been his last birthday and I won't even be there to celebrate with him.

"Eight decades. Good for the man. Do you want me to drop you?"

Should I check my hearing or did she just say that she will drop me?

"You want to drop me?" I point to my chest. *Me?*

"Yeah, if that's okay with you. Or maybe I can give you my phone to call someone to pick you up from here."

I don't think any of my family members will travel for one hour to pick me up in the middle of nowhere. Missy would but that would include a bunch of things she wants me to do for her and I am not interested to deal with her now.

Every birthday with Grandpa is important, I knew it since I was a kid.

"I don't know." I say, unsurely. He would be upset if I didn't come but he would understand. Grandparents always understand.

"It's the man's eightieth birthday and you are his grandson. It would make him upset if you are not with him as he blows the impressive 80 candles. Or the 80 with 8 and 0 digits, that would be easier and save breath."

She does have a point. I can visit grandpa, ask one of my friends to pick me up and take my car with the tow truck in the morning.

Also, I get to have a car ride with freaking Aria of the Celestials. I can talk to her about my band and maybe she could agree on meeting together.

She didn't seem that uptight with a helping hand she has given me so I can give this a shot.

"Thank you for letting me come with you."

"Mention not." She keeps the toolbox back in the trunk and gestures me to come.

Aria sits on the driver's seat, buckling up. I do the same.

She raises her eyes at me in question.

"Did you lock it?"

"Lock what?" The seatbelt clicks.

"Your car." She says it matter-of-factly.

"Oh shit." I undo my seatbelt and jump out of the Mustang. I lock my car and check all the doors are securely closed.

I sit back in the car and I see Aria smiling at me, amused.

"What?" *Do I have something on my face?*

"You're dorky, you know that?" She answers, her smile increasing a little.

I furrow my eyebrows. "Is that a compliment or an insult?"

"A compliment, definitely. Dorky is good." She starts the engine which sounds way better than mine and passes me a lingering look. "Dorky is cute."

Warmness spreads to my chest.

The car starts moving but I can barely feel it when I am flying on marshmallow clouds.

We drive in silence. "Hey, can I ask you something?" I pique.

"Yes, you can."

"I feel anxious in silence. Do you mind if I play some songs?"

She doesn't answer me but I see a hint of smile shadows her lips. She takes her phone from the dashboard and holds it out to me.

An iPhone 14, white color. The screen lights up and the wallpaper in her picture with three more girls. Her band.

The girls are glowing with happiness. There is a huge crowd of fans behind them.

"That was our first time touring." Aria says, noticing me looking at the screen.

"Wait, you're a singer?" I ask with fake astonishment.

She laughs freely. "Not meaning to brag but I belong to just the best girl band in the world"

"Your word or theirs?" I squint my eyes playfully at her.

"Mainly mine." She admits but she's just being modest.

"You look happy." I comment, swiping an absent minded thumb over her face on the screen. She has one of her hands in the air, another one over the shoulder of her band mate. I don't remember her name though.

"Well, having your first show sold out on your first tour does wonders to your smile." I smile at her comment.

Seeing her smile makes me smile.

"Your password?"

"271001."

"Complicated."

"My birthday."

"How very daring."

Aria laughs. "You should see my house's password then."

"What is it?"

"It is…" She stops, a purposeful smile plays on her lips. "There's no way you are getting the passcode, creep who I picked off the street."

"Is that how little you think of me, Aria?" I tsk, disappointed.

"So you do know who I am."

"I never denied it." I pointed it out and she considered it.

I open the Spotify app and press the library icon to check out her playlist. As I scroll through them, I admire her song selection. She really has a good taste in music.

But I still search for my favorite songs. Before I press play, turn to her seriously and say, "I know that you might even know this masterpiece because this was way before you were born, kiddo but it would be a privilege to introduce this masterpiece to you."

"Ha, try me."

"Okay, I am gonna try you." I mimic her, putting the song on. The phone is connected to the car system through the Bluetooth so it starts playing in the speakers. She frowns as the intro plays. Some ol' wind rustle and guitar riff but the moment the first lyric comes on with a thunder, she already figured out the song.

'All the leaves are brown
And the sky is grey'

"California Dreamin'. Seriously, dude?"

"How did you hear this?"

"Because it is the most amazing song ever. The Beach Boys is the level I try to reach. They were brilliant."

"I should have guessed that you are a Beach Boys fan." I mumble and slump into the seat.

"Too bad you didn't." She looks over at me. And she is smiling. An involuntary smile breaks out on my face.

Her smile is so infectious. And here I was, a foolish guy standing in this disease ridden area of confusion with no mask, no sanitizer and no Lysol, plain out open and waiting for her beautiful infection to take me in and infect me whole.

"Take a right from here." I pan my right hand to the direction I wanted Aria to take. She takes the right. "Straight down the road and second house to the left."

"Okay, Google maps. Shut up." She waves me off as she scans my neighborhood with familiarity in her eyes.

Has she been here before? She might as she was coming to this place. Maybe a family to visit.

It was almost on the tip of my tongue to ask her about what happened in the conference room earlier that day but I stopped myself. I don't want to intrude on her personal matters. Also, I had fun with her on the drive over. More than I ever had talking to a person for the first time.

And the conversation flowed so easily. I have never felt so relaxed with a girl before.

"We're here." She puts the car in the parking mode right on the side of the curb. I turn to the right and there it is. My grandpa's two story house, lively as ever.

"I am sorry to make you drive all the way till here. Hope you didn't have any important work."

"Nah, I don't have any work, let alone important work. I just sit around on my ass all day." She jokes.

"I find that hard to believe but okay." I chuckle. "But are you sure that I didn't keep you away from something?"

"No, *Callen*, You did not." She emphasizes. My name rolled off her tongue and it was agonizing.

On the drive down here, she asked me my name and I couldn't lie or cover up my identity. I was scared to tell her because she would have recognized it from her 1pm meeting she was supposed to have but she showed no sign of recognition. Also, there was no way she saw me in the waiting room, she was engrossed too much into whatever the emergency was.

"Okay, thank you, Aria."

"You're welcome, *Callen*." I unlock the door and step out. I lingered at the door.

"Hey, can I ask you something?"

She gives me a warm smile that would make the sun ashamed of itself. "Yes, you can."

Now is the time. Ask her about the appointment. Pitch her your band. There is only one chance.

"Can I have your autograph? My grandpa is a huge fan of yours." I sputter out, already banging my head internally over the stupid decisions I make in my life.

"Sure, I would love to." She lets her hand wander in the backseat before pulling out a roll of paper, I think.

I peek into the car to see the paper and it is actually a poster of Celestials.

"You keep your band poster in your car?"

"I was supposed to sign it before it went to shipping so I try to squeeze in how many I can when I have breaks or in a car ride to the studio or meetings." She opens her glove compartment and takes a marker out.

"Signing posters during a car ride. Now that's multitasking."

She smiles, signing her name in the poster. Hair curtain one side of her face as she is signing and I resist the urge to push it behind her ear.

"What's your grandfather's name?"

"Edward."

"Grandmother?"

"Minnie. Why?"

"I low key hoped that it would be Bella but life has always been tough on me. Here you go." She rolls the poster back and hands it to me.

I take it. I can't believe that I have a signed Celestial poster in my hand and that one of their members drove me all the way to my grandparents' house.

"I better get going." Aria says, checking her watch and then at me. "It was nice meeting you, Callen."

Stop with the demolishing butterflies in my stomach, Aria.

"It was nice meeting you too, Aria. Thank you for the ride."

44

"Mention not." She winks and the jelly feeling in my knees returns, wanting to knock me off.

I slam her door shut and she waves a bye before taking down the road. I stand in the same spot, staring as her Mustang takes a right on the intersection and disappears.

I wanted to invite her inside but she obviously had some work delayed because of me so I didn't disturb her further.

The poster was in my hand, I rolled it open and I saw their previous album photo-shoot. It was a club look with a halo effect on the walls. They are in dresses, matching the theme, black and purple.

The other three girls have already signed the poster. Zeenat, Lexa, and Ver. Aria's was the one with the recent ink.

Dear Edward,
Celebrate everyday like it's your birthday.
Congratulations on the big 80.
Love, Aria.

Chapter 8

ARIA

"And I told him, why don't you take your third class camera and stick it up your ass." Lexa is telling her story of pap trying to seduce her and how well she handled it.

Zeenat laughs weakly, and my heart clenches at it. I hated seeing her like this. Bed ridden. A large stitch on her head is surrounded by fat bandages and an IV.

I remember what Mom used to say.

Bad things always make a way to bring us down and it's predestined to be that way but you have to develop coping mechanisms because no therapist in this world can pull you out of the hole unless you don't want to come out yourself.

So every time you feel like you are on the edge of the cliff, try remembering all the good things you had in your life and how many more you can have. Backtrack from that cliff while you still have a chance because once you fall down, you will keep falling down.

I close my eyes. What am I grateful for?

My dad, my memories with Mom and Astra, the girls who are my family, my fans and my life.

My phone rings and I open my eyes. Kate is calling.

"Who is it?" Lexa asks. Ver and Zeenat's attention turns to me too.

No work talk. That's what we decided on the car ride over. Zeenat worries about the most about our work, second to me. With her injury and almost a month before she is cleared out for work, I don't think she can handle that we are not allowing her anywhere near our meetings and the studio.

"A guy I met." I blurt out.

"What? You met a guy?" Zeenat asks with surprise. Her eyes show life for the first time since the accident.

"Umm, yes." Guilt thunders in me for wanting to lie to her, but look at her; she looks interested in something rather than pretending to be interested in it in Lexa's stories.

Ver palms his face, and Lexa twinkles with amusement.

"Who is he?"

Don't get your hopes too high, Zeenat.

"A one-night stand."

"Oh." And just like that, she dims.

"A one-night stand you gave your number to?"

"Seems more than a one-time thing to me, Ari." Lexa comments sneakily.

I throw her a warning glare.

"Yeah Ari, it looks more than it." Ver jumps in.

"Please shut up."

"No no, tell us more about this guy." She pushes on.

Kate calls again and Lexa takes the cue even though there is none. "See, he is so impatient. Can't wait to hear your voice. Are you guys gonna have phone sex?" She teases.

"Screw yourself. Hard." I sneer at her.

"Is that what he did to you last night?" Zeenat jumps in their hooligan wagon.

47

"Not you too. I am just going to go and call someone, which is not that guy. You guys have your food."

"Yes Mom. Would you like a tissue box? For cleaning up after the *activities*."

"Dude." I make a face at Lexa. When I am out of the room, I call Kate back.

"You know what a blow on my ego it is when my boss doesn't pick up my calls." She says, answering the call.

"What is it, Kate?"

"I know that you are busy with Zeenat, and I am sorry to disturb you at this time of tragedy, but ma'am, you have so many people to attend to. The board meetings, calls from producers, and Mr. Suxxen Also, Hayes called. He wanted to know when the sessions for the new album started.

"Can you hold the fort a little longer? Zeenat needs us."

"You know I am trying my best." I sigh. "I will come back to work tomorrow. Just keep Mr. Suxxen on the schedule. Later on, I will talk with the board."

"Can I get a time?"

"Sure. 11 AM. Tell the board that I will be there."

"Okay ma'am. What about Hayes?"

"I will call him on my own, don't worry. I need to finalize things with Mr. Suxxen beforehand. Cross check it with the board, and then only I will get to Hayes."

"I will inform him of that. Thank you, ma'am."

"No, Kate. Thank you. You have been a huge help since these 3 days. Bear with me a little longer."

"I will, ma'am. See you tomorrow."

We say our goodbyes and I cut the call.

Tomorrow is going to be a busy day.

"Good morning, Miss Aria." He greets me as I enter the room.

"Morning, Suxxen. Care for a coffee?"

"I would like that."

I press the intercom and Kate answers.

"Yes ma'am?"

"Two decafs, Kate."

"On the way, ma'am."

"Okay so let's start discussing?" I ask Suxxen and he nods.

"Before we start, miss, I would like to let you know that I am sorry about Miss Zeenat."

"Thank you, Suxxen. She will be joining us in a few weeks."

"I am looking forward to meeting her." He dips his head respectfully, and I think that not every first impression is a lasting one. Suxxen came off as a cocky bastard at first to me, but he is actually a good man.

"About the band schedule, I was thinking to start with this year first."

"Yes miss. As you said before, you want to launch a new album this year."

"Correct."

"Do you have an idea in mind?"

"I want this to be fresh. A mix of everything. Not a heartbreak album or a seasonal album. I want anyone to hear this album and relate to it. I want this to be about our happiness, freedom, and ups and downs. This album can be about…life. A celebration of life."

"Never done before, I like it." He writes it down on the paper. "How long will it take for the album to be written?"

"Four months. Two months for choreography, shooting music videos and photo-shoot."

"Okay." He jots that down too. "After that?"

"Three or four months for promo. Talk shows and a few performances. Then we tour."

"Which places?"

"I would let you and Niya decide that."

"Anyways, we are in June right now. This year will pass with the album. If we take 3 months to do the promo, I would say an April or May concert would be good."

"What about we start it mid-April and finish it by, let's say, 20th May?"

"I like that. Let's go with that."

We continue back and forth planning and soon, we have decided one complete year of our band.

Suxxen takes a picture of all the dates and ideas he jots down and sends it to me. I forward that to the girls so they have a look too.

"Meet you at the label's building?" I ask Suxxen. My back is stiff from how long I was sitting down so I rise up to stretch.

His eyes widened at my question. "Wait, am I supposed to come?"

"It would be fair if you do come. You're our artist manager after all."

"Miss, it would be a huge honor."

"You can call me Aria, Suxxen." and I have never seen a man smile that big and happier ever before.

Chapter 9

CALLEN

"C'mon, Kate. Help a man out."

"I don't want to." She crosses her arms, relaxing back on her chair.

"Please. Just tell me where she is."

"Hmm." She makes the sound as if she is thinking but then shakes her head ruefully. "No, thank you."

God, Aria's assistant is so stubborn.

"Pretty please."

"Not even with sugar on top."

I called Kate the weekend after Grandpa's birthday to ask for an appointment but she denied. Apparently, Aria is taking a week off for some emergency.

No matter how bad the curiosity killed me on what the emergency was, I was scared. Scared that I will never get a chance with her. To show her what I wanted to. I needed to keep reminding myself that the band was the reason I wanted to meet her and not the magnetic pull I had with her last week.

I had to focus on bigger things, whether I wanted to or not.

"Please be a darling and tell me where she is. I have been asking for an appointment for the past month. Only to get 5 minutes with her and that is not even happening."

"Why do you even want to meet her so bad?" She tilts her head curiously.

"Because I want to pitch my band to her and make her to listen to our demo music. Please Kate, we have to chase our dreams." I plead with her.

I think Kate is a big believer of dreams because the stubbornness in her eyes reduces.

"See, I can't tell you where she is because of confidentiality issues." And my hopes crash down. "But you seem like you really care about your band and I think Aria might give you a chance so why don't you give me your demo and I will make sure she listens to it."

Just like that they soar back up. "Really?"

"Yeah but I can't guarantee that you will get signed with a label or get to hang out with the Celestials but what I do know is that Aria is a believer at heart. If she feels like your band has potential and that you are a good person, she will go head over heels to make things work for you."

"Thank you so much, Kate."

"It's alright." She smiles at me and I am so grateful for her.

I give her the demo CD of Corruption and she jots down my phone number on a sticky note so she can contact me with any update.

As I step out of the KVN building, I let the unbelievably happy tears out with a laugh. I can't stop grinning as I sit in my car.

I think my dream might finally come true. I think I can make it with my band.

I drive off the parking lot as a black Jeep enters it.

Chapter 10

ARIA

The meeting was going way better than I planned.

Suxxen and I were a great team and we were killing it.

"6 months for one album? Isn't that too long, Aria?" Amber asks me like I was planning to keep a baby 12 months in my womb before giving birth to it.

"I honestly don't think it's too long. We are right on track."

"But Celestials finished writing their last album and shooting it within 3 months. This album is taking double the time." Megan presents the fact.

"I am aware of that, Megan." Time to get real and play the cards right. "But you know things are not going great for us right now. With Zeenat's accident, we are missing a vital member. Also, I know that our last two albums were made fast but that is because we wanted to."

"And you don't want the third album to be the same?"

"No, we don't." I see Suxxen wince from the corner of my eyes. *Be truthful, just tell the truth.* "These two years have been a rollercoaster. In the next two months, we will be celebrating 3 years of Celestials and I am so proud of who we are. But I feel like we should take a step back and slow down a little. My band is my family. I hate to overwork them. I hate to push them harder when they are already pushing themselves beyond their limits. I hate being tough on them when they are the most amazing and talented girls. So I know that this isn't how we have been from the past two and a half years but this is the repo and pace we are setting for ourselves now. I hope all of you understand it."

My mom always believed a person can have all their principles and rules that they set for themselves over their life but if you talk to their hearts instead of their belief system, they will hear you and they will understand you. Her thoughts would confuse me. I asked her how she was so sure. And she would answer me in her warm voice that never got irritated with my questions or their lack of depth.

Because we all are different in our beautiful ways but there's two things that bind us together. Love and humanity. If you love someone enough, others have that much humanity in them to understand that. No one is cruel, dear. No one.

"We understand, Aria and we give our condolences and support during this time." Amber says genuinely.

Mama was never wrong.

"What about Zeenat? Has she gone public with her accident or is planning to keep it undercover?" Meghan asks.

"Right now, no one knows except us. She is in a hospital which is a public place and even after the bodyguard we stationed for her, I still don't feel comfortable with her being there after people know about her accident. So after she is discharged from the hospital, we will let her take the reins and do whatever she prefers. Either tell or keep it to us, we are leaving it completely to her."

"A sound and well planned decision." She agrees. "About the album, how many songs can we expect?"

"I would say 8 but it depends on our writing process right now. But we won't exceed more than 10."

They ask a few more questions and I answer them off with Suxxen's help.

"Well, I think that's it. Thank you for coming, Aria. You too, Max Suxxen." Amber gives him a handshake and a hug to me. "I am excited for the third album and give my best wishes to Zeenat and the girls."

"I will. Thank you, Amber."

I met the rest of the people in the room and it's the same thing over and over again. Excited for the album and wish Zeenat good health.

I smile and nod my way through hugs and handshakes till I am out of the conference room.

"Wow, people really love you." Suxxen comments. He was waiting outside for me.

I give him a tired smile as I swipe my blazer off, neatly folding it, I turn to him. "Well, Suxxen. It has been a good day."

"A very good day, miss."

"Aria." I correct him and he smiles.

"Sorry. Aria."

"Yes, a very good day. It would be good if you take a day off tomorrow. Enjoy with your family."

"Really? The kids will be very happy." He bows thankfully and leaves. I think I see a hop in his step.

The man hops a lot. I checked the time on my phone, 5:00pm. Kate must be wrapping up her work so I decide to pay her a visit. I took the elevator to her floor and as I guessed there she was, hastily typing something on the keyboard.

"Busy day?" I ask, leaning on the wall and she looks at me, startled.

"Oh hey, didn't see you there. Hi."

I push myself off the wall and go to her desk.

"Seriously, has it been a busy day?"

"Every day is a busy day when you are the assistant to a successful band."

"Thanks for the compliment and sorry for making you work this hard."

"Hey, hard work pays off right. In my case, by the big bucks." She flaunts, wiggling her shoulder. We do pay her a lot. Not your average PA.

"Got that right."

"By the way, how was the meeting with the label?"

"Nailed it." I sing falsetto and she claps excitedly.

"I know you would nail it."

"Thank you for your faith in me." I put a hand on my heart.

"That's why you hired me. Because of my good ol' faith." I smile, walking back.

"Good night, Kate."

"Night, ma'am."

I press the elevator button and it takes a few seconds for it to reach my floor. After hopping into it, I go all the way to the parking lot.

Just as I open my car, someone shouts behind me.

"Ma'am! Ma'am!" I whipped around to see who was causing a commotion in a nearly empty parking lot in the evening.

Kate comes running towards me.

"Kate, is everything okay?"

"I forgot to give you this." She is panting as she hands me over a CD.

"What is it?" I ask, taking it off her hand. The CD was a black one with white letters written, *CORRUPTION*.

"Just hear this. If you like it, tell me."

"Kate, explain to me what's going on."

"Please, just do this for me. Believe in a dream."

"Kate–"

"No questions asked!"

"OK, OK. I will listen to this. Just breathe."

She nods painfully. "Yeah, I will work on that." She waves me off, going back to the building and I am left with questions and concern.

She will be fine, right? She looks like she would be fine. I start my car and keep the CD on the passenger seat, eyeing it curiously. *What do you have in you to make Kate run 5 floors down to the parking lot?*

My car system beeps with a new call as I drive on to the street. Lexa was calling.

"The meeting went great." I answer the call with.

"I knew it! We can always count on you to get us on track."

"Suxxen was a great help."

"I knew that too! God, I am on fire tonight."

"No fire, Lex."

"It was a metaphor. I am not that dumb."

"Yeah, I am well aware of where the meter stands. How's Zeenat?"

"Better. She went to the washroom without fainting."

"Big step."

"I know and she wanted to write today."

"It's always 2 steps forward and one step backward."

"Yeah. She really insisted on it. I saw her writing lyrics on the napkin and scatting in her sleep. And you won't believe this, Mr. Hot Coat thinks it's a '*good development*' Zeenat is showing interest in her daily life routine and we should encourage her more. What does he think he is? Mr. Hot Coat?" Lexa sounds completely flushed.

"If Cameron thinks that this is good then so should we." I lecture her. "Also, please don't eyeball Z's doctor, we need that guy."

"He does have a big, muscular crotch. That means he has a big, muscular you-know-what."

"Alexa Sangria!" I scolded her.

"Sorry! He is just too hot."

"I don't care. Keep your eyes to yourself, young lady."

"OK." She replies monotone.

"Good. Do you want me to come over to the hospital?"

"Not at all. We got everything under control here. Anyway, it's Ver's turn to sleepover. I will be home by 8."

"You sure you don't want me there?"

"Very sure. You need rest and even if you do come here, Zeenat will ask you many questions about work. We really don't want her to have any stress, right?"

"Right." I wanted to be at the hospital with them but Zeenat was a questioning 4 year old. I really couldn't risk telling her our busy schedule till she is healthy enough.

"Meet you at home then."

"Love you."

"Feeling is reciprocated." I tease her.

"I'm sure it is." Lexa cuts the call, laughing.

I reach our home and park my car in the garage. Gathering all my things, I lock the car and unlock the house door.

I was greeted with emptiness. Trying to shake the feeling off, I close the door behind me and go to take a shower and a much needed change of comfortable clothes.

After I am done, I get down to the kitchen and to the liquor cabinet. I really needed a relaxer. Half a glass of red wine normally does the trick.

As I pass my living room, I see the CD tucked in my blazer, I pick it up.

Kate wanted me to hear this. I have no idea why but she did. Maybe she made a band called Corruption? Not a clue.

I took my wine and CD to the studio that was the only place we still had a CD player at. I press the eject button and the tray slides out. I slowly take the CD out like a newborn baby and place it on the tray.

It starts playing.

"Hello, listener. This is us, Corruption." A male voice speaks an insanely good one. The one that involuntarily gives you tingles.

I hear the guitar strum up and click of drumsticks. "One, two, three, four." Someone says before they start playing.

I recognize the song as 'Every Breath You Take' by The Police.

As they sing, my mind and body relaxes. This is the most beautiful version I have ever heard of this song.

I am left sitting on the hardwood floor, amazed beyond the depths of my wine glass on how amazing they strung up the song. Their voices. *Oh, their voices.*

I pick up the telephone we have in the studio and call Kate.

"Hello?"

"The band is amazing. Who are they?"

"Wait, you like them?"

"Uh huh, I do. Who are they, Kate?"

"Only your next best thing!" She hollers happily through the phone.

Chapter 11

CALLEN

"One, two, three, four." I count down and we start playing. The air fills with the starting tune of our song.

I gather my mic in my hand as I start singing.

"Running in the front,
We are running away from everyone
Look at us,
We are burning with passion
We will win one day
Night and day, we are going to make it.
How we conquered the sky
As long there's life in us,
let us fly high
Whoa oh oh, we will"

I stop and so does the music.

"What will we do?" I asked the boys and they gave blank looks.

"I have no idea." Cade admits, slinging his guitar behind and taking the lyrics sheet.

"Don't we have to be famous to be writing a success song?" Edwin adds.

"That's stupid." Andrew shakes his head, tucking his drumstick in his pockets.

"But common sense." Edwin retorts back.

This launches a full blown banter while Cade reviews our lyrics for our new song.

We are finally emerging a bit out of our writer's block and started writing songs.

Cade and I were the songwriters of our group. He was doing most of the writing; I have not been that productive recently.

I take my electric guitar and sit on the couch, experimenting with the strings.

I was 11 when I first listened to music. Yeah, I heard jingles and rhymes before but not real music until that night.

My dad played a song for my mom, Elvis Presley's *Can't help falling in love*. My mom sat on the special chair which was really just red bed sheet draped over our dining chair with a ribbon Missy used for her school project. He played on the keyboard, singing and Mom was smiling from the chair with tears in her eyes.

Dad has sung to Mom so many times over their marriage but I remember that day so well. I was sitting on the couch with Cam and Missy, grinning from ear to ear as the beautiful scene unfolded in front of me.

I learned two things that day. Music is a gift I want to create and love is so darn beautiful.

"Hello? Yes, this is Callen's phone. May I know who this is?" Andrew talking pulls me out of my thoughts. I raise my head to see him on my phone.

He covers the phone's speaker with his hand and whispers at me. "It's a girl."

"Which girl would call him?" Edwin voices my thoughts and I don't even take offense.

"Yeah? Give me the phone." I make grabby hands and he throws them at me, I catch it.

"Callen speaking."

"Finally! Am I supposed to go through an army before I get to talk to you?" I recognized Kate's sassy voice immediately.

Kate.

Aria's assistant Kate!

"Hi, Kate!"

"Chill there, will you? My parents don't greet me with that much enthusiasm, let alone demo-handing freaks." She hushes and then pauses. "Okay, I just heard myself."

"Kate."

"Yeah?"

"You know why you called."

"Rush much?"

"Please, Kate. Don't make me beg."

"Yeah, I am not doing that anymore. You did it enough when you were in the office."

"So?"

"Sooo?" She elongates her O's, teasing. Kate sure did love basking in suspense.

"Kate!" I yell impatiently.

She pauses for cinematic effect.

"SHE LOVED YOU AND WANTS TO MEET YOU!" She screams over the phone.

An unbelief gasp turns into a scream in my mouth.

Oh my god, oh my god, oh my god.

"Hey, hey. What is happening?" Cade claps for my attention as I start jumping on the couch.

"We are meeting her! We are meeting her!" I jump off the couch and catch Cade's hands, hopping in excitement.

"Meeting who?"

"I don't care; I am joining the happy hopping circle." Edwin drops his guitar and comes squealing at me. He catches my hand, and Cade's springs with me too.

"Aria from the Celestials." I holler happily.

"No ducking way!" Andrew joins the happy hopping circle and we jump happily. We are finally getting to meet her.

Another step closer to who we want to be and the future we always imagined would be.

We are going to leave our legacy, our mark.

Chapter 12

CALLEN

Edwin shakes his leg nervously.

"Edwin, stop."

"I am nervous." He cries out. I instantly feel bad. I know his anxiety takes control during situations like this. I really can't blame, only help him.

"OK OK, cool down. Ed, why don't you roll down the window and take a look at the scenery?" I advise, trying to calm his nerves down.

"Okay." He slides to the window on his side and looks at the pedestrians.

With Edwin's attention away from us, Cade is the first one to voice his apprehension. "It is just not him who is feeling edgy today."

"I know."

"Self-doubt is wrecking me right now, man." Andrew scratches the back of his neck. He looks flustered with his gray shirt clinging on him. We all were in formals because even though the first impression doesn't last forever, it is still important. "Now that we got a chance, I feel like we might screw it up. How are we so sure that Aria is our ticket to get signed by a label?"

"I actually searched it up." I pull my phone out of the pocket, handing it over to them. "Aria is a major shareholder at the company. She delegates, that's for sure. But she still is a very important person there. If we impress her we will get into the label, no matter what the other person says."

Andrew and Cade check the phone. "She is our key"
"She is." I agree.

"Just one person to impress which will be fine."

"I wouldn't be so confident. Aria is a singer. She is in a band that even a 5 year old knows about. Heck, even my dad knows about them. Just imagine how much she and her band mates have done to be in the position they are right now. Number 1 on all platforms."

Cade catches what I am trying to say. "They have seen the world." *And we are mere village in front of them.*

"What should we do then?" Edwin's attention is back to us as he stops looking at the window.

"First thing first, we should be bold. We should be positive. We should have faith in ourselves and the band. If we don't believe in ourselves, no one else will. We are slowly emerging from our writer's block so we will write better songs soon. Last but not goddamn least, please don't curse or say any weird things in front of her. Be charming. We are not only good in music but also good in manners. Right, boys?"

"Right." They say in unison.

Edwin looks out of the window again and he taps me furiously with his face glued to the window.

"What?"

"Look." He points outside. We all huddle towards the window and my jaw drops at the view outside.

A mansion–*a very huge one*– is in front of us. The black iron gate, which was as tall as a house, slid open gracefully and the car moved in.

65

A large fountain is in the middle as we circle it, the grass is manicured so clean. If I spend a whole day just looking for flaws in this garden, I would be unsuccessful. It was *perfect*.

"We are here, sir." The driver announces, stopping the car.

To our left, the most magnificent mansion that this land could have ever seen stands like a proud heiress. The exterior was sleek and stylish like it hopped out of an Elle decor magazine and made home here.

We were speechless as the driver opened the door for us. A motor function kicked in and scurried the boys out. My feet landed in the ground and the electrifying jolt went through me.

The aura that surrounds the mansion was buzzing. Positive and up lifting. I have never felt like this before.

"I have informed Ms. Lexa. She will be there to meet you soon."

Andrew thanks the driver and we proceed to go to the front door.

Cade exchanges nervous looks with us before pressing the bell. A loud chiming echoes through the place.

Why does it feel so scary yet exhilarating at the same time? The door swings open and I see the girl who I have seen once in a concert and countless times in billboards, Lexa Sangria.

"You must be the band." She greets us with a cheeky mischievous smile.

"Yeah, we are. It's nice to meet you." Andrew steps up like he is the manager of the group and shakes her hand. But O dear, does it stop that much? No, no, it doesn't.

He holds her hand delicately and kisses it. Lexa's cheek turned to a shade of pink at Andrew's shenanigans and I wanted to yank him. It was a clear rule. Don't mix pleasure and business together.

"Why don't you come in?" Lexa says, stuck in a trance. Then she realized that she is only inviting Andrew, not the rest of us. She flusters, "Come in, all of you." She pushes the door even wider if that's possible and gestures us in.

I step in and look around, wondering if I should remove my shoe or keep it intact. I preferred it on. What if my socks smelled?

"Don't worry, you can keep it on." Lexa says as she closes the door and leans on it. "It is a rule for us to remove our footwear as soon as we are at home, not guests and visitors."

"Who set that rule?" I ask curiously.

"The mother of the house, Aria." She chuckles to herself. "Talking about the mother of the house, let me call her down." Lexa gets off the door, typing something in her phone. "She'll be down soon. Have a seat."

We sit on the sofa. I thought their sofas would be soft and unbelievably soft because when you can afford luxury, why not? But they were comfortable and not harmful for your backbone yet expensive looking.

"So let me introduce myself. Hi, I am Lexa. I like singing, dancing and making bad decisions so I made it into a career. What about you guys?"

"First of all we are huge fans of you and love every song. We are the Corruption. That's our band name. And we were thinking that you and your band members, the Celestials could guide us through the music industry. We just wanted your views on something that could help us launch our career." Cade says.

"Well, lucky for you. Aria is the right person for this, dare I say, the best. She is a total queen of revamping trends and style, ideas that no one has ever seen before and her marketing strategies have never proved us wrong." She praises her friends like she was the sun in her sky.

Her expression turns serious. "Just because she knows what to do doesn't mean that she will do it for you. Show her that you are the right band. Show her that you're worth it."

"She sounds hard to please." Edwin mumbles to himself.

Lexa picks it up with her bat-like ears. "She might come off like that but she isn't. That girl has a heart of gold and never backs out in helping anyone."

The sun in her sky.

I hear metal whirring somewhere. I turn to see an elevator open. A freaking elevator in the middle of the living hall and two girls, one scarred at the corner of her head and other supporting her with an arm around her.

"There they are." Lexa cheers. The girls make their way to the other side of the couch while the girl looks like she is healing from an injury, heaves a tired sigh as she sits.

"That is Zeenat, the sexy minx," She gives us a tired smile. "And this is Ver. I think you might know her boyfriend, Cash."

"The Cash Flow?" Cade asks with wide eyes.

"Yeah, he was a big fan of economics in college." Ver sighs. Something tells me that she is not a fan of her boyfriend known as The Cash Flow.

"See Niya, we would love to tour through Monroe but we really want to live longer." Another person's voice.

But this is familiar. Familiar as in she fixes your car and hitches you a ride to your grandpa's birthday and then signs a poster for you.

My palms start sweating at the thought of meeting her. Coming face to face and she realizes I am the same guy who she helped. What if she thinks of me as a creep? A stalker?

Footsteps echo the stairs. *She is coming down the stairs.*

Lexa is talking about something and all I can think of is what Aria will think of me.

"Stop being so stingy, Niya and give us a tour bus. You know it will be so fun. We will let you drive too." She laughs as she says it. "Just consider a tour bus, that's all what I am saying."

She rounds the stairs as she enters the living hall. The first thing I noticed was the easiness in her. She had an easy and naughty smile on her face, dressed in a pajama which looked like something that a person would wear on a Christmas day for opening their presents but the way she pulled a red checkered pajama at this time of the day shocked me to my core.

Aria registers people in her living room. "I have visitors. Call you later, Niya?" She says into her phone. "Yes, yes, I will think about it. Bye."

As soon as she is done with her call, she faces us with a bright smile.

"I apologize for letting you wait. That was our tour manager." She walks over to us. Her eyes scan the whole living room and when they see me, she nearly trips over her legs.

"Whoa, are you okay?" Lexa reaches out a hand to catch her.

"Yeah, yeah. I am." Aria regains her posture and smiles on her face. "Sorry, the carpet is a little tilted." Her eyes don't leave mine.

"Mary! That woman has another lecture coming from me about carpet tiltation. Do you even know how hazardous it is, Aria?"

"It's absolutely fine. Leave it for now." She soothes Lexa's hand and turns to us. "Let me get a chair from the dining hall."

I look around the living room and see only two more empty seats. One was a recliner and another was beside me.

She comes back hauling huge ass chair in her hands and sets it in front of us. With smooth flow, she slides into the chair.

"So let me start by introducing myself."

"Oh, we know who you are. Big time." Edwin blurts it out. I glared at Edwin. We were supposed to keep our cool. Aria doesn't get weirded out but actually smiles at his comment.

"I know but it makes me feel good when I introduce myself. May I?" She asks his permission and Edwin chuckles. He is already put at ease, I can see that.

"Sure you can, sorry for interrupting you."

"No worries. So where were we? Introducing, yes. Hi, I am Aria Bastian. This is my band." She flaunts the girls like they are her proud masterpiece. "And I hope you got introduced to them. We are the Celestials."

"Happy to be at your service." Ver bows comically.

"Absolutely correct, Ver. We are." Aria gives a genuine pointed look. "I hope you can give a little info about yourself because honestly, Kate, my assistant, was so secretive about you all so I would really like something to know."

Cade does the introduction for us. "Umm, so we are Corruption. I am Cade."

"Edwin."

"Andrew." He throws in a hand wave.

Aria acknowledges all of them with a nod before she looks at me. If it was the first time I met her, I couldn't decipher her expression but I had a one hour drive with her, I could read what her face held. *I remember you but I am showing everyone that we are total strangers who never met before letting them know that we jammed to Doja Cat's newest release a month ago.*

"Callen."

She sucked in an inaudible breath like she knew it was me but considered me as a mirage till I spoke out. Our eyes lock and refuse to move. "Hi, *Callen.*"

There is that jolt again. She says my name and an electricity judders in my body. Only by saying my name, she can make me feel like I am in a thundercloud. I would most probably short circuit when I am in closer proximity with her.

Lexa notices our little interaction and nudges Aria by her foot. Aria snaps out of her trance and so do I.

"Hi to all of you too. Cade, Edwin and Andrew." She backtracks. "Let's get down to business, shall we? What is your purpose for contacting me?"

Simple and to the point.

The boys look at me in a swift move and I am put on the spot. *Be bold, be confident.*

"We are your typical garage band. We made Corruption almost 4 years ago and played it at almost every school, bar, and club in our area. But at the end of the day, there is a feeling. It is like hunger—a need. To have more, to grow, to make our music available to everyone who will love us."

"You want more? Doesn't that make you greedy?" Aria rests her elbows on her thighs, looking at me with curiosity and amusement.

Cade turns to me, skittish. I didn't look at him but at Aria. She is really putting me on the spot. Like she is challenging me.

"I am not being greedy. I want us to go there into the real world."

"There is a sufficiency in the world for man's need but not for a man's greed."

Did she just quote Gandhi to me?

"It's not greedy when you work hard for what you want. No one *needs* to be famous, but they *want* to be famous. A human's needs are limited by survival, but the desire to leave your mark and a legacy in this fast-paced world is what we are truly capable of. The world would have not been what it is now if everyone were happy with their needs fulfilled. And maybe I am greedy because I want everything that I can work for. No cutbacks." I heave an aggravated sigh as I finish talking.

71

The guys glaring at me like I was doing with Edwin a few minutes before. *I lost my cool, shit.*

With my heart beating the losing beats, I turned to see Aria's reaction because I know that I have already lost this meeting off my hands. She bites people's heads off in the conference room. I saw the end result myself when I was in the waiting room of her label.

Aria surprises me again when I see her smiling at me. She gives an approving nod before she proceeds on the next question. "Normally when you give your demo to a band, you expect collaboration. Is that what you want?"

I pull my flailing pieces back under control before answering her question, "We want guidance. We have no idea how to present ourselves. We don't know how to approach the label. We just thought that maybe you could help us."

"Okay, that's not bad, we can help you boys out, don't worry." Lexa waves us off like we gave her an easy task.

"Yeah, we are always glad to help people in the music business. If we musicians don't look out for each other then who will." Ver nudges Zeenat.

"We are happy to give you any advice that might help you." Zeenat voices her agreement.

They look at Aria.

"We will help you out. Gladly." She tells us, but eyes don't move from mine.

She has claimed them forever.

We spent the next hour in their house. A maid, who I guessed was Mary, bought us tea and coffee, and got scolded lightly by Lexa on the carpet topic.

All the girls were very friendly. Even Zeenat who retired to her bed after a while because she wasn't feeling well. My gut feeling told me that Aria's emergency was related to Zeenat and the scar on her forehead.

Soon, it was time to go and we were bidding them goodbye on the entrance.

"The driver will be here soon. Wait for a while." Aria gets off her house telephone and tells us. "Callen, can I talk to you?"

I freeze. *Dethaw before you embarrass yourself.*

I smile, "Sure."

She walks forward and I follow her right behind her.

"Let me guess, your friends don't know about you hitching me a car ride?" I ask.

"No, actually. Even your friends don't, do they?" She slows down to my stride.

"No."

"Get hitched by famous people much?"

I laugh. "No, you're the first."

"Glad to know." A possessive tone hints at her voice or did I imagine it?

"I didn't tell them because they would have been pissed at me." I reveal.

"Why?"

"Because we were trying to get an appointment with you for so long. If I told them that I spent one whole hour in your car with you but didn't ask about our band, they would go ballistic."

"You got a poster for Edward so it's a win-win, right?"

"Yeah, it is." I say nonchalantly but my head keeps screaming. *She remembers your grandfather's name!*

Silence befalls us as we walk in the soft grass. I get to admire the manicured lawn even more closely now and indeed, it is flawless.

There is a nagging feeling in my chest since I spoke out about that greedy topic with Aria. I was so rude and

73

selfish; I really didn't want her to think of me that way. "I am sorry for talking that way with you. I didn't mean it."

"I did see the culpability in your eyes after you said it. But the thing is, Callen, you don't have to be sorry. I like it that you prefer working for things rather than getting it handed to you by your personal workers."

"Believe me, I do not fall in that category." I scoff. I was a kid who grew up on repeated clothes and recycling jars.

"My point is that as a person who has worked hard for what they stand on now, I know what you are talking about. And there is nothing bad about playing local. Stepping stones are out there and you will climb it. Everyone has a quiet time before the waves pull you in and you are in a whirlpool. You are on your own time; enjoy it while it lasts because sweetie, it is exciting and confusing in here."

"You mean our time will come?"

"Yes, it will. But if you want it to come, you can't sit in your garage waiting for your big break. If you play small, you stay small. It's okay to want more, do more, and be more. You would never float in your whirlpool if you don't dangle your feet near the shore."

"You're right."

"I am going to talk to a few people and see what I can do."

"Wait, really?"

"I said that I will see what I can do. No confirmations yet. But yeah, I want the world to see Corruption and don't you think that it would be good if we took a step towards that goal?"

"Aria, this is such amazing news. Thank you." I throw my arms around her, hugging her. I am levitating with happiness.

It wasn't until she patted my back that I realized that I hugged her without her permission.

Her face is redder than mine. "Sorry, not much of a hugger. But hey, congratulations in advance." She bumps my shoulder.

I smile at her. She looks so dorky and cute like this.

Andrew blows a whistle, calling me over. A black car parked in the front.

"I think the driver is here." I point at the car, dumbly. As if she needed any instructions of seeing a black SUV.

"Yeah. Have a safe ride."

"Thank you. Bye." I turn on my foot to walk but she stops me.

"If everything goes well, can you and your band come up with a song in one week?"

"We can try." I know it was a long shot but not a no shot. With a potential label signing fueling us, we will certainly write a song.

She might have understood the look of trepidation in my face because she softens her angelic face. "Don't worry. I know you guys will do great."

"How can you be so sure?" I ask, barking out a weak humorless laugh.

"Because you don't have to be in Vegas to bet on casinos. I can see it in you. You have a knack and fire for this. I am betting on you, Callen and I know there's a pot of gold on your end." She looks nothing but genuine.

My chest is still trailing with sweet, warm honey as I sit inside the car. The car drives out of the mansion and the boys high five themselves over the success of the meeting but I could only think of the sweetness in my chest, the warm eyed girl and her words that made me more confident than I have ever been about myself.

I am betting on you, Callen.

Chapter 13

ARIA

The boys didn't fail me at all. I am yet again in the conference room for the KVN Label, making the them listen to Corruption. Their reactions included touched smiles, extra approving nods and happy tears.

'When you believe' is indeed a beautiful song. I expected them to give a pop or metallic song. It seemed like their genre but yet, this was another lesson for me to not judge the book by its cover because they can write an emotional song and make you tear up slightly on your white fluffy bed.

"Who are they?" Amber asks, wiping off a tear from beneath her glasses.

Work your magic, Aria. Get Corruption their deal.

"They are this really good band called Corruption. They originate from Minnesota and played at many local bars and clubs. Their voices are so original, the auto tune is put to shame."

"But they are not exposed to anything, we have to put a lot of work into them." Megan presents. She presents her questions a lot. "It's raw talent, Meg. We mold them the way we want and I know you can use a new and fresh group." I state with conviction and confidence.

Amber and Megan exchange a look.

Come on, give me what I want.

"We love them!" Amber claps her hands excitedly.

A huge weight relaxes in my chest.

"Thank you, Amber. They will not disappoint you." I intend to keep my words.

I wrap up all the work for their contract and leave as soon as possible after we set the appointment for signing tomorrow morning.

First person I can think of calling was Callen.

But then I stopped. Won't calling be too personal only to tell about the contract?

When he talks, he gets all my attention. *All.*

I have never been so interested in talking to some random guy but I just met. Well, not exactly 'just' met. I did give him a ride to his grandpa's house.

A car ride, nothing else.

I shut my eyes as I think of another meaning of ride and my body reacts by pointing my nipples hard. I restrict any more images. Business is business; I can't let my mind wander somewhere.

So I pull him up in my messages and give him a text.

Aria- Hi! *You have a meeting with the label tomorrow morning. Dress sharp. I will pick you and the boys up at 8am.*

Callen of Corruption- *Can you hear me screaming?*

Callen of Corruption- *Aria, this is great news. You're amazing!!*

Callen of Corruption- *Wait, let me tell the guys.*

Callen of Corruption- *Hahaha, can you hear them screaming too?*

Callen of Corruption- *We will be ready tomorrow.*

77

He follows it up with his location. I drop the phone in the car console and start driving. I catch a huge smile on my face through the rear view mirror.

Chapter 14

ARIA

I honk for the third time, casting a frustrated look towards the house on my right. A small, well maintained house whose residents were supposed to be ready at 8am and it's already 8:10. I was on time with breakfast bagels and planned to get them coffee on the way but they could have coffee only if they actually step out of that damn house.

My patience is wearing thin so I honk for the fourth time and the door flies open seconds later and a guilty looking boy band with top unbuttoned shirt and tousled hair spills out. My annoyance skyrockets at their tardiness but damn, they looked good.

Callen moves into the back seat with Edwin and Cade. Andrew sits up front. They shut the door and a string of apologies weaved by their unpunctual mouth.

I ignore and don't even give them an ounce of attention as I pull out the car from the curb.

When they realized that their whines were affecting me as much as a barking dog would, they became quiet.

"We really didn't mean to be late. Edwin snoozed the alarm." Andrew covers up.

"For the hundredth time, I. DID. NOT." Edwin yells and they start arguing like little kids.

Men are truly the foolish descendants of monkeys.

"Enough!" I shout, throwing them an angry glance and they zip up. "Not only did I work my butt to get the label to sign you guys but I am giving you a ride to a building. The least I would expect from the four of you is that you could be ready on time. That's *all* I asked."

"Sorry, Aria." Four voices say in unison.

"I am not trying to be harsh but I need to know that you guys understand the gravity of what you are going to do. This isn't some gig you played, this isn't your garage. This is the music industry. If you are late, you lose. If you take things for granted, they slip out of your hands. You should maintain a standard for yourself and make it higher, year by year, achievement by achievement. There is no place for slacking."

"We were just 15 minutes late." Edwin mumbles from the backseat.

"And what does that say about you? What if we get traffic on the way and miss the meeting? What will you do then?" I answer him through the rearview mirror. "Just tell me honestly, do you want this opportunity or not?"

"We do want it." Callen emphasizes strongly. I hear the desire and a hint of desperation in his voice. I look at him through the rearview mirror and he is already looking back at me, eyes flaring with determination.

He looks completely opposite of the way he did the first time I met him. The boy who was funny and shy, belting the lyrics to California Dreamin' is the same one who was looking at me fiercely with promise.

I turn my eyes to the road to be accident prone and somehow stop the cartwheel my heart is doing is my chest like a show off dancer.

"Don't repeat it next time. I am not a fan of tardiness."

"What gave that away?" Cade says, laughing.

I hand them bagels and they basically inhale them. It never occurred to me how boys can eat. Is the size of their mouth bigger than girls for chewing food? Does their chewing and tongue moving the food from one side of the mouth to another differentiate between people? I wonder how big Callen's mouth is? What about his tongue?

My eyes widen as my train of thoughts switches tracks to an explicit station.

I focus on driving and the way to label's building.

In 15 minutes, we reached. There is only 10 minutes to spare before the meeting starts and knowing Amber and Megan, they can be in the room even half an hour before the appointed time.

I give the car keys for valet parking and leave the man with a list of instructions and 'be careful' warnings. I was using Ver's Audi today because she is the only one in four of us to have a car with more than 2 seats. Rest of us had sports cars, convertibles, jeeps and what not. So I borrowed her car because I had to accommodate five people in a car including me and my Mustang doesn't allow that.

The boys walked behind me, surprisingly matching my quick strides. We pile into the elevator. I turn to them, I have a good 25-30 seconds before we reach our floor. And I want to utilize the time to give them a few last minute pointers.

"Be confident. Be cool. Don't fidget, don't keep shifting in your seat." I was about to say, don't sweat, but I notice Andrew. I hand a Kleenex from my purse to him and he gives a thankful smile before wiping beady condensation on his forehead and neck. "There is no way you can present yourself if you don't know what your worth is. Even if you lack self-confidence, its fine. I will put you guys in therapy later, but for now, fake it and fake it good."

Cade raises his hand. "How should we fake it?"

"Think about The Kardashians subtlety and Machine Gun Kelly's openness about his relationship. Does anyone want to hear about it? No. But does that stop them? Not at all. Carry their traits."

"I want to be Khloe." Edwin butts in and Andrew nods. "Oh, you're definitely a Khloe."

Edwin's chest swells with pride at the compliment.

"Yeah, choose whichever sibling you like. But exert power and confidence. Also most of the board members are women because this is a female management label so use your boyish charm and sexiness."

"Isn't that manipulating them with our looks?" Andrew asks with a small frown.

"Yeah but you guys have the goods so show it off."

I purse my lips in embarrassment as soon as the sentence finishes off but they just laugh.

"Don't worry, Aria. I got the goods and I know how to use them." Andrew does a funny dance with his impressive crotch.

Heat creeps up my neck as Callen's smiling eyes look at me provoked by my mishandled comment and his friend's stupidity.

I give them some more precautions and *do's* and *don'ts* before the elevator door opens.

I spot Kate in the waiting area with a bunch of files in her hands.

"Good morning, ma'am."

"Morning, Kate." She hands me my coffee and two files as we make our way to the conference room.

"Oh I forgot to tell you. Book a studio for 2 hours. We just wrote a song last night and want to record it today."

"Yes ma'am. Do you want Stonecutter?" Kate asks, referring to one of the recording studios.

"No, go for Gravity. I prefer them more."

She types in her iPad. I glance at the boys, making sure they look presentable and they were. My eyes linger extra long on Callen.

"Are you ready?"

They all nod, excitedly.

I can see the happiness and nervousness in their eyes. They did deserve to go out to the real world, show what they have and my heart swells to be helpful to them.

"Good luck for the meeting." Kate wishes the boys and I see a small nod exchanged between Kate and Callen.

"Thanks, Katy." I turn to enter the conference room. Callen comes beside me.

"If they like us and sign us, remember that you made our dream come true." He whispers and a warm blanket drops over me at his words and his close proximity.

"Believe in yourself, Callen. Good things await." I wink at him and the sweetest smile pulls on his soft lips. That is an image that is not going to leave my head anytime soon.

I was more than determined to get them the deal. For him.

I take a deep breath and push open the glass door and I can smell the Axe body spray cloud follow me.

Chapter 15

CALLEN

We all walk out with the biggest smiles on our face.

Nothing feels better in the world than signing a paper, confirming that you are a part of KVN Label. They told us if we would like you to sign to the same record company as Celestials and we agreed.

Cade throws a bear hug around me and even though I am not a hugger, I let him have this one.

"We took the first step to our success."

"We did!" I pat this back, happily.

Andrew and Edwin who were hugging each other come and hug us and it's a group hug.

As we break off, I see Aria leaning against the glass wall, a small adoring smile on her face. I want to give her the biggest thank you for her. I was just a random boy who she went over the fence to help.

I honestly had no idea that she would come this far and get us a label deal. I step forward to her with a grin to thank her but Andrew reaches her first, hugging her and lifting her off the ground.

My heart drops a little as I miss my chance.

Aria suddenly looks uncomfortable, patting Andrew's arm repeatedly telling him to put her down.

"I'm sorry. I didn't mean to overstep the boundary." Andrew apologies as he quickly sets her down.

The discomfort on her face eases as she dusts her attire, a black shirt and white pants, off. "No no, it's fine. It's just that, I am not much of a hugger."

"Wait really? So is our boy, Callen here." He motions toward me. "You both should date." He says with earnestly.

I choke on air. That bastard.

Aria's sweet melodic laugh echoes the empty waiting room. "Don't get your hopes up, buddy. He is just a friend."

"Girls and boys can never be friends." Andrew imparts wisdom.

"They can be when the guy doesn't want to stick his thing in the girl." I retorted.

Aria gasps mockingly. "That sounds a lot like you, Andrew."

"Hey, I am just saying. Sexual attraction happens. Boy is horny, the girl is hot. Things happen."

Aria shakes her head. "Someone make him a biology teacher."

She presses the elevator button to summon the metallic box. Her hair whip as she looks at us over her shoulder. A mischievous smile is broadening on her face.

"Come on guys, I have a surprise for you."

It's a 20 minute drive to whichever place Aria wanted to take us. She is in a better mood now.

Morning was our fault and we got to see her *no-excuses-needed-from-your-sorry-ass* side which, to be honest, was sexy and scary at the same time.

I was half compelled that she was going to ditch our ass on the side of the road because why not?

But she tolerated us and I am happy that she did because there was no freaking way we could have gotten a record signing us this morning.

She really is an angel in disguise.

"We're here." Aria announces from the driver's seat.

I peek out of the window to see a tall building. An apartment building maybe?

Aria guided us through the front door and I was met with luxury on my step in. The air carries an utmost class and the whole lobby is decorated expensively.

We are met by a woman at the reception. Her face lights up as she sees Aria.

"Good afternoon, Ms. Bastian."

"Afternoon, Ellen. Thank you so much for clearing your schedule for this."

"It is my honor, Ms. Bastian." The woman says genuinely, keeping a hand to her heart and bowing her head slightly. She raises to see us. "Oh, you must be the ten-"

"Ahh Ellen!" Aria rings off a warning and Ellen closes her mouth quickly.

"Oh, they don't know?" Aria laughs a little at Ellen's shaken demeanour.

"No, they don't know yet. And if you don't mind." She gestures expectantly forward and with whatever they both are hiding, Ellen picks up the hint and nods sheepishly. "Yes, Ms. Bastian."

She leads us to an elevator and we pile in. Our bulky bodies make a wall and Aria stands with Ellen in front, chatting away.

Cade taps Aria's shoulder softly and she turns her head to him.

"Yeah?"

"Where are we going?"

Her lips curl into a sly smirk. "Oh, you have to wait for it."

"Please." I say involuntarily.

Her eyes size me up deliciously and she takes her sweet time, lingering for a longer second in some places.

"A surprise loses its essence if revealed too soon, Callen."

My name. Her seductive tone. Her pink tempting lips. Her gravity pulling eyes. Her sweet smell.

The elevator door opens and she moves out, taking her divineness away with her.

Ellen opens a door with a keycard and hurries us in. I come to a slow stop as I take in the place around me. It's a penthouse.

Lush black leather sofas, expensive decor greets me. One wall is completely made of glass and the view looks so terrific with a promise of looking even better during the night time. There's an open kitchen with a marble counter. Lights shaped like snow globes hang down. Stairs led up to a floor up which looked like an open office. Nothing about this place was homey. It was dripping with luxury.

"Aria, where are we?" I rotate to her and see her bend over the counter with a pen in her hand.

"Your apartment." She replies without looking up. Edwin, Cade and Andrew freeze, mid-exploring.

"What?" Andrew bellows

Aria meets our eyes. "Your apartment. Okay, discussion time. Either you all share a penthouse or take separate apartments. We have two penthouse and two suites right on the floor below. What do you say?"

"I would say you're joking." I utter in disbelief.

"I am not." She answers, shrugging. "It is the perks you get to be signed to a record. Accommodation given by them and as you can see, it's not an ordinary apartment."

"So we can have a whole suite for one band member if we want to?"

"Yes, you can. I have reserved 5 apartments for you because I didn't know what you guys will choose. FYI, the fifth apartment can be used as a home studio."

We all exchange a look. This was a huge thing. We need to go do round table conference to decide whether we wanted to live together or separately. It is as important to us as our cereal brand.

Aria, magically, seems to interpret our looks and politely tells Ellen that we will inform her later and sign the lease.

Ellen congratulates us and leaves.

We are still taking a tour of the penthouse which is going to be under our names, Aria calls us from the kitchen.

"A little of what is going on in here. I have an official signature on your lease because having my sign gives you advantages like the minimal rent for your profession as possible. When you decide what you want your living arrangements to be like, give me a call and Ellen will bring up your lease to sign it yourselves."

Cade reaches out to catch her hand. "Thank you." His voice quavers a little.

She says nothing but keeps a reassuring hand on his. She understood how he felt.

Overwhelmed. Sad about how fast the days passed since you were a 10 year old who played drums for fun. And happy to finally reach to this point of life and wanting to scream out of the rooftop that you made it.

"Also, after the record likes your song, they give you money. It is an estimate of what they think you would get from this one song. And you are a freshly signed band so they give a bit extra too, like a bonus."

"Really, how much is it?"

I was expecting a maximum of $1,000 or even less than that.

She again signs something in her checkbook and tears it off, handing it over to me.

I plucked it out of her impressive manicured fingers, nervously.

The boys huddle behind me as I stage the check in front of me. At first glance, I see 1000 and I am happy.

This is good, really good. This money could go in his savings account for the house. I can save up for Missy's abroad year. I can do so much, even if they split the money, I can do so many amazing things.

I realized this was my first paycheck. Sure, we got paid for gigs and I worked in fast food joints but this was my first check. Something I worked hard for. So did the rest of my band. I was floating on air to correctly see the numbers on the check.

Shit.

It wasn't 1000.

It was 10,000.

Ten thousand dollars.

Before I opened my mouth to speak, I heard a thud right behind me. We whip to see Edwin passed out. Most probably after knowing that he is going to get his share 2,500 dollars all for himself.

Who won't faint at that amount?

Chapter 16

CALLEN

Being a singer is exciting, exhilarating and exigent at the same time. It's been 2 days since we recorded our song, '*When you believe*'.

Being in a studio was really fun. When I stood in the live room, it felt like the world was suspended from me. It was me and my voice and the tune playing from the headphones. I sang my heart out, I gave my best because it would be a cold day in hell before I lack or give up on the most important thing in my life.

Chase, a 30 year old man, was our producer. We were pure amateurs and couldn't sync with tune when we were in the studio because we were not used to referencing our voice through the headphones. The pitch was also a problem for us. But he guided us very well.

Today, we did the last finishing touches and the song was sent to the management for a listening.

We had many meetings, photo-shoot scheduled, hours with the campaign director to kick start our career and in all the chaos, I still haven't met Aria. I obviously didn't expect her to babysit us but I thought that she might have been involved in the process a little bit but she wasn't.

I let myself fall face first on my bed and let out a tired groan.

I and the boys decided on separate apartment for us, I and Cade were on the top floor and Andrew and Edwin took the suites for themselves.

We meet every morning at Cade's penthouse for breakfast because he has more experience in cooking than we three collectively do.

My mobile rings and I let out another groan, turning to my back.

I pick up to see the screen illuminated by Aria's name. She is face timing me.

I launch off the bed and fix my hair quickly. After that only I pick up the call.

"Hey!"

"Good morning, rock star. How is the singer's life treating you?"

I nearly want to cry when she asks that question. "It's tiring."

"Aw, honey." She smiles knowingly.

"Do we really need to spend an hour deciding on our song cover? It seems too much."

"Obviously you do. The song needs a cover that matches its vibe. Example when you look at the aging picture of the Weeknd, you know we are talking about his album, Dawn FM. Cover carries identity, Callen."

"I know but it takes an hour for that?"

"Be happy that you choose yours in an hour. We took one week to decide on our first album cover."

"Oh, *Break Me*'s album cover is an artistic masterpiece." Their first album, *Break Me* is a picture of a cracked angel flying upward but her legs are tied down with chains.

"Exactly. Masterpieces are not born, they are worked hard on."

She imparts little words of wisdom whenever they talk. She is very responsible and mature for her age. There is a whole population of 20 years olds who know only 4 things. Get drunk, drug, sex and fucking their lives up.

Aria certainly didn't belong to that group.

In our call, I see her walking somewhere. I can see the straps of her tank top and a Tiger cap secured on her head with wireless ear buds plugged in her ear.

"Where are you right now?"

"I went to the gym and I am walking back home right now."

"Don't you have cars? Like millions of them?"

"That is so not true." She acts offended. "I just have 43 cars, not a million."

I bark out a laugh, lying on my bed. I stifle a yawn.

"Are you tired?" She asks and I am not even shocked to hear her concern. Aria is a therapist and sunshine rolled into one. One look she takes on me and she knows what I am going through. Either she is a really good face reader or I'm an open book.

"A bit." I downplay it. Last thing I want her to do is get worried.

"Callen, I don't know what to say. The whole thing is bittersweet. You need to work hard to get the life you planned for yourself but if you work too hard, it's not good for you."

"It's just the starting right?"

I see the sorrow in her face. "Yeah, it is. But every beginning is hopeful. The story will go the way you want it too."

"Isn't the writer the one who decides it?"

"Not if the book is character driven." She points out and I smile.

I note down her saying, be character driven, not plot.

"Don't let fate decide what you want to do."

Aria smiles, her face fills my memory. Absolutely correct."

"It's on YouTube."

"Spotify too."

"What about Apple Music?"

"There too."

I relax back on the sofa. Our song is released on YouTube, Spotify, Apple music and Deezer.

"Guys," I say in disbelief. "Our song is out. Our *first* song is out."

There is a moment of quiet.

The soaking in of the moment.

We have officially released our song. It's out there in the world. And people will hear this and if they like it, they like us. They become our fans and we become their go-to music.

My phone pings with a message but I am too into my trance to pick it up. A minute later, it pings again.

"Oh my god, you won't believe this." Andrew squealing, jumping off the sofa, breaking me out of my trance.

"What is it?" Cade asks.

"Aria just gave a shout out to our song."

"Wait, are you actually serious?"

"Yeah, look." He shoves the phone in our hands and we check it out.

She posted a video of herself captioned with *@corruption's new single, When you believe, is OUT NOW! Go check out their amazing song!*

Cade presses play on the video and Aria's bubbly voice floats through the living hall.

"Hi everyone! Tonight is a very special night for me because as you know, we got nominated for 2 Brits awards which I would take a second out of and thank every person, every Celestial Being out there who supported us. We are truly grateful for you all! Also, the other reason why the night is turning out to be amazing is because my dear friends, The Corruption have released their very first single, *When You Believe*. Go check them out and stream their amazing songs. I cried when I heard it and so will you." She winks at the camera as if telling us, *look boys; I'm going to make you popular.*

"She has 500k likes already and the comments look really promising to us." Cade says, grinning as if he got an A + in his test.

"Aria is amazing. I can't believe she did that for us."

"Actually, a shout out from a worldwide famous singer is the biggest promo we can ever have." Edwin turns to me. "Thank her, Callen. She's an angel for us."

"I will." I take my phone and see two notifications from her. One is the Instagram notification of her tagging us in her video and the other one is a message.

Aria- Congratulations, Callen! Celebratory dinner for you and the boys is on the way.

Callen- I'm intrigued. What is it?

Aria- A bunch of seafood. I hope that no one is allergic to shellfish.

Callen- Nah, we are pretty generous here.

I cringe at my own joke. Shellfish as in selfish. Opposite of selfishness is generosity. *Oh god.*

She sends two laughing emojis.

Aria- I'm sorry. I haven't been much involved in the process. Your first song is a huge deal and I should have been there to celebrate it with you. Sorry, Callen :(

Callen- Hey, don't you dim your mood. You're the reason why we could have even released the song in the first place. The guys call you angel.

Aria- Good to know that you have no hard feelings.

Callen- Never, Aria. Never.

Her text bubble appears after a pause. I texted her with a more serious sounding message than I intended too. So I shot her again.

Callen- *Thanks for the shout out. We all appreciate it.* Especially me.

The text message from her comes easier and without hesitation.

Aria- *Just doing what I can* ❤

Aria- *The dinner has arrived. Open the door.*

Right on the cue, the bell rings. The chatter stops and everyone's head turns to the door.

"Were you expecting someone?" Cade asks.

"I bet there is no girl behind the door." Edwin teases.

"When is there ever a girl behind the door?" Andrew retorts.

"Can you all shut up? Aria has sent over a celebratory dinner. For us." I announce, opening the door. People dressed in black and white enter the apartment in a line with colorful dishes in their hand. I see various crabs, fishes, shrimps and prawns with buttery dips.

They arrange it on the table and file out without a noise.

"Aria, you're an angel!" Andrew shouts at the ceiling with his hands high and jumps off the sofa and to the dining table.

"Sir," One of the waiters tapped my shoulder.

"Yeah?"

He hands me a bouquet of flowers. "From Miss Aria." I thank him and close the door behind him.

There is a white note standing out from the fragrance and color. I pick it out and read it.

Dear Corruption,
You have started your journey into this music industry. I hope this is the first of every flower you will

*ever get from your adorned fans. I am very first to join
the Corrupted gang.*

Love, Aria

My cheek hurts like someone is pulling them. But
when I catch a glimpse of myself in the mirror and I am
smiling so hard.

Chapter 17

ARIA

Always making the headlines
But you have no time to go home
Your parents await
Your brother just scored a goal for his team
But where are you?

Everything was a dream
When you wake up against the odds
You look here and there
Not knowing where you are
Your footsteps betray you
But there is no one left to love you

Can I wake up now, from this terrible thought
This world doesn't mean anything
when you're not there next to me
It was up to me to save all what we could have been
Can I wake up now
Can I go back to who I used to be

Nothing will keep us apart
You're my family

I climb the crescendo on the last word and drop it.
Then it's time for the chorus.

Can someone wake me up from this dream
(I'm dreaming, I'm dreaming)
Can someone turn back the time
(Turn back the, turn back the)
Can someone love me back to life?

An emotional chord struck with the last line and I am
glad with it.

The girls did an amazing job in the chorus.

Hayes is too stunned to speak as he starts clapping
slowly and then picks up speed. Soon, everyone in the
opposite side starts clapping with him and I bask in their
applause, smiling.

I remove the headphone and hang it on the mic.
Bending down, I take the water bottle set beside the mic
stand and gulp it down.

After me, Vera and Lexa will record their solos and we
will be done for today.

Our writing process has always been very calm. We
write what we feel like, we sing how we want and keep the
process repeating till the day we are supposed to choose
the songs for the album.

In our last album, we wrote 15 songs and recorded 12
in which only 8 made the cut.

We never felt like restricting ourselves in a box or
writing for a target audience. We write what we feel and
they are people out there who relate to us. Because in this
messed up world, more than one person goes through the
same shit.

I turn to put the bottle in the dustbin and my heart leaps out of my chest when I see a face on the door window looking at me.

Andrew's smushed face.

I gasp at the sight. He drools on the window. Someone pulls him back and opens the door. Callen's gorgeously annoyed face greets me and winged creatures soar in my stomach.

"Hey. Sorry about him."

"I don't even want to ask what he is doing."

"Neither do I know what to say." He laughs. "I am sorry. We wanted to meet you and Kate told us that you will be here."

And yet Kate didn't inform me. But maybe she did and I forgot to check my phone, I have been flanked with work the whole day.

I motion Hayes f I am done here and he gives me a thumbs up.

"Let's go on the other side of the box, it's more pleasant there."

"You don't have to tell me. It is crampy here and you have to ask for a chair when your legs get tired, they don't give one to you already."

"Downsides of making music. But hey, at least it's a profitable business." I comment and he grins at the mention of it. I signed the group's check before it went to them. 12,000 dollars each member. "How do you feel?"

"It was a huge surprise. Edwin fainted again." He jokes. "I can't believe we have done all this."

"You really put yourself out there. You deserve what you got."

His eyes soften. "Thank you, Aria."

We got into the studio. The rest of Callen's band and my girls were talking with each other.

Andrew spots us first, he came back here when me and Callen were talking in the live room. "Yoo, Aria. The song was so cool. Gave me the chills."

"Thanks and boy, wash your tongue with Purell, you were licking windows. I don't even know if they clean it well."

"Aria, you were amazing!" Cade boosts me up.

"Seriously, how do you keep your vocals so good?"

"Olive oil, not shouting too loud and no drinking."

"Singer's rule to live by." Lexa bumps my hips. "But baby, you struck a deep nerve in there. Love it."

Callen and I sit down as Lexa goes to her solo in the live room.

Zeenat and Ver were with Hayes, helping him change the tempos and coordinate the vocals. I would join them too but I need some time to replenish before I carry on.

I pull a chips packet from the snack basket and pass it on to the boys.

"So you wanted to talk to me about something?" I ask Callen, popping a chip in my mouth.

"We did. I hope we are not keeping you away from anything important."

"Not for now, carry on."

"Well, Cade had this crazy idea."

"I am more of a visionary, Aria. I prefer to look and develop for the future." Cade shrugs like that's how he is built. "But I got this great idea which will help us immensely and you too. Help me, help you. A little Logan Paul vibe right?"

When I don't laugh at his comment because the joke was so old, he continues. "I have a proposition."

"Many people do."

"You see how much of an amazing response we got for our single. One million in 5 days. I never could think we would get such a huge response."

"Yes, congratulations for that." I say unsurely. I have no idea where Cade was going with this and I didn't want to be rude in any way so I let him continue.

"Our producer, Chase, told us that you tweaked the audio a little before approving it."

"I did that." I finally got a hang of what might be going on here. "I know I should have cross checked it once with you but I got to listen to the audio an hour before it got uploaded so I couldn't send the changes to you guys."

I look back and forth on them. I am not the culprit here.

"Oh no, no. We love the changes you have made. The people love the beat drop and the last tune was brilliant. I can't believe we didn't think of that." Callen covers up, soothing me.

"Then what is the problem?"

"The problem is," Edwin says "that you're amazing."

I let out a relieved laugh. "Thank you?"

"No, seriously, you're amazing. You know the nooks and corners, front and backs of a good song, and the music industry. You are a guru."

"What is the point you're trying to convey?"

"That we want your help."

"My help in what?"

"For making us a new album."

"What are you saying?" I am ready to dismiss the idea. It sounds so stupid.

"Listen, Aria. I know we asked for a lot when we asked you for listening to our demo CD but you got us signed to a label. Got to release the professional way and gave us a shout out that bumped us up. You're clearly a pro. Please help us make our album."

"I can't. I really can't. I am a singer myself. I have the same hectic schedule you do and maybe more busy. Why should I be making your album when I have my own band's album to be written?"

"Aria, please."

"Just give me a reason why. Tell me why I should double my meetings and schedules when I am perfectly stressed out with one band?"

They pause, racking their brains, coming up with a plausible explanation before Andrew goes out of his way and says, with a pout, "Because we're your friends."

"That's the dumbest reason I have ever heard." I retorted.

"What if you don't have to double your work?" Callen speaks up.

"What do you mean?"

"What if you don't take care of two bands but only your own yet you help us too?"

"How?"

"Help us when you're free. Listen to our music and give back suggestions. Give us the instructions and numbers of people who we are supposed to contact. Rest of it, leave it to us. Just be a guidance coach. Guide us down the right path." He says dramatically with a cheeky grin.

I stare at him, deciding what I should do. I could have said no to Cade, Andrew and Edwin but Callen. What does he need to be so handsome and thoughtful at the same time?

My excuse sounds dumber than Andrew's.

"Please, Aria. We need you."

"Just help them out, Ari." Ver says from the sounding board and it pushes my mind to the right direction.

"This album only. After that you guys are on your own." I announce and they cheer out so loud that Hayes nearly falls off his chair.

Callen hugs me. I am suddenly aware of every single atom of my body. His hands snaked over my left shoulder and connected to my right shoulder. His breath tickles my ear. The feel of his hand on my body and the smile on my skin.

He pulls apart and is too shocked to understand what just happened in the cloud of happiness and goes to rejoice with his band mates.

Ver, Zeenat and Lexa from the other side of the glass look at me in shock and amusement.

I shrug because I myself had no idea what to decipher of that.

102

"So, Aria. How should we contact each other when we send you audio? Will email be fine?" Edwin enquiries.

I regain myself and answer with a smirk. "Oh honey. We don't half-ass things here. I go all in when I take responsibility for something."

Ver takes the opportunity to make a crude joke. *"That's what he said."*

Chapter 18

ARIA

"Where is everyone?" I opened the door thinking the band is on the other side but only Callen greets me, all alone.

Callen hesitates at my question, his Adam apple bobbing as he answers, "There might be a little problem."

"Which is?"

"They are still at home."

"I specifically told you guys to meet me at the studio at 10am. Why aren't they here yet? If you had any transportation issues, you should have let me or Kate know so we could have arranged something." I can feel my head weighing.

"Transportation wasn't exactly the problem, their health was."

"What? Are they sick?"

Callen was struggling to break the news slowly to me. "More like a hangover."

"You gotta be kidding me." I mutter, rubbing the temples of my head.

"I did tell them to quit drinking and go to sleep. But they wanted to celebrate the new release and that you said yes to helping us out, so they kept going on. I'm sorry, Aria." He sounded sorry and embarrassed over his bandmates behavior. The bags under his eyes showed that he didn't sleep well either. I wasn't going to get angry at him for his bandmates mistake. I wasn't such a bad person.

"Did you have breakfast?"

"Huh?" He is quizzed by the sudden change of topic.

"Did you eat before you left home?"

"Um no. I was in a hurry to get here." *At least someone was.*

I pick up the receiver at the corner table and call the front desk.

"Hi Catalina, this is Aria from studio 10."

"Good morning, Ms. Bastian. What can I do for you?"

"I would like you to send 2 chicken subs to our room, please."

"Okay ma'am. Would you like a beverage to go with it?"

"I would take a 7up diet." I cover the receiver, looking over my shoulder at Callen. "What would you like to drink? Pepsi or coke?"

"But it's 10am in the morning."

"Say what you want."

"Iced tea."

"And one iced tea, Catalina."

"Okay, Ms. Bastian. Will bring it right up."

"Drinking 7up in the morning isn't good." Callen says as I keep the receiver down.

"Nor is being on an empty stomach so far into the day. We all have our vice and virtues, Callen."

I pull a chair from the recording panel and sit down. "Care to join?"

105

Callen makes his way to the other chair and sits down. I notice his calves with more interest than calves are supposed to get.

"What do you do in Corruption other than singing?"

"Write songs."

"Are you the only songwriter in the group?"

"Cade is too."

"What do Andrew and Edwin do?"

"They both are good in choreography but Ed is better in fashion."

I jot all this down. Over the last few times I have met them, I did notice Edwin's weird but bold outfits. I liked them.

I'm still thinking how we should plan up their album when Callen speaks up.

"I have a book in which I write songs or scribble lyrics on. Would you like to see it?" He sounds embarrassed for some reason.

"I would love to see it! Show me." He hands me a black spined zebra print thick book.

As I see the songs, I am in awe. They are so good. They were original, had a deep meaning and were so catchy.

"I can write something else, if you don't like them."

"Are you kidding me, Callen? This is brilliant. You're an amazing songwriter. Especially this line," I read a line from his book. *'Let your colors blind their eyes, do what makes you feel alive'* and this *'We're running out of time, we are running from each other. Baby, please pull me back before I go too far'*. I really like them."

His face glows at the gratification.

"You think we can go ahead with this?"

"Obviously we can. But can I throw an idea at you?"

"Shoot."

"We both know that this book is a gold mine but what if we brainstorm now? Come up with music and beats for now."

"Live in the moment right?" He agrees.

"Right." I bite my lips to prevent myself from smiling. Most people would dismiss or look weird at me whenever I say tacky sayings. Callen encourages and agrees with them rather than thinking that I grew a second head.

"So let's do it." I put on headphones and gave him one.

My hand hovers for a second over the music panel, blankly.

"It's all about experimenting." Callen says, leaning a little on my side.

He lifts the knob up and a synth wave plays through our headphones. Then he presses a few keys on the color board. A beat starts playing and it's pretty cool. He adds a few more times and I find my head moving with the time he just made.

"That's cool."

"Oh yeah? Listen to this now." He moves his hand once more over the panel and duck quacks are added to the music.

I start laughing at the ridiculous tune.

Callen starts rapping.

My name is Mr Duck
I live by the mother erk
I quack everyday
They say I quack here, I quack there but they don't
know that I am gonna quack this world up
Listen up, kids. Let me tell you a story.
It's about the OG duck
The Mr duck
He roamed the streets
With his bling bling
He gave the people his middle ring ring
Who is he? (Callen)
The OG duck (Aria)
Who is he? (Callen)
The OG duck! (Aria)

107

We burst into fits of laughter.

"You should become a rapper." Callen controls his wheezing and wipes the tears away.

"You're not bad either. We should release the song together. It would be hilarious."

"Just imagine the merch we could sell with this. I already have so many ideas."

"A T-shirt with duck in sunglasses, a golden chain and a cap."

"A backward cap."

"Absolutely. And we can sell biscuits for a limited time too."

"In the shape of a duck. Hey, we forgot one thing." He says with all seriousness and I instantly know what he is going to say.

"OG Duck bath bombs!" We say in unison and our eyes widen in surprise at the jinx.

We again start laughing.

"Ahh, I don't think I've ever laughed this much in a long time. My sides hurt." I wince as I breathe slowly.

"You should do it more often. It looks good on you." Callen says.

That's when I feel how close we are. He has his elbows rested on his knees, bent forward. I was sprawled over my chair which was touching his chair.

Humor leaves his eyes as he takes me in. His eyes travel downwards from mine, escalating my body. He gulps when his eyes land on a strip of my skin. My shirt must have ridden up when we were laughing.

He darts his tongue over lips, wetting them and suddenly I can't breathe.

A knock on the door makes me jump out of my chair.

A man, dressed in pure formals, enters holding a tray.

"Your breakfast, Ms. Bastian."

"Oh. Um-keep it there, please. Thank you for bringing it."

He places the tray on the table and leaves with a respectful nod.

I turn to Callen and he is looking at me with an unreadable look. What just happened was way too intimate.

Fuck, this has never happened before whenever I wrote music with anyone.

"Breakfast rolls?" I smile cheekily at him.

"And that's a wrap." I say, checking the time.

"Are you sure? We can do a little while more?"

"No, I already kept you in here long enough. Our session was supposed to be for 2 hours. Look at the time. It's 2 pm."

"Time flies."

"Like a hummingbird."

"Are you sure we can't work a little more?"

"Callen, I woke up at 5am today. Please let me have a few minutes to rest before I have to go for vocal practice."

"Sorry."

"I didn't say it to get your pity. Also, how are we going to proceed without singers? Singers sing. Basic knowledge, Callen."

"We could have done so much today. Only if they weren't hung-over."

Callen seemed to be the eagle of the band. Taking care of schedules, band practices. He's like me but a mild tyrant. If the girls had a hangover, I would have still pulled them out of the bed, blasted loud music in their ears and would have not given them sunglasses so they could get a migraine from the sun.

Just thinking about how the boys missed their studio session makes my blood boil.

Tardiness is my pet peeve and god, does it peeve me off.

"I'm dropping you home." I announce getting up.

"I can book an Uber. You really don't need to."

"I can and I will." I am already off the seat and making my way to the door.

"Am I in trouble?"

"No, the rest of your band is."

Chapter 19

CALLEN

This is going to be so entertaining.

Aria has a thing with people being late and I totally saw that during the car drive to KVN Label building. But when the person doesn't show up at all? Boy, all hells are breaking loose.

"You take the noodles and I will take the rice."

"Yes ma'am." I unplug my seatbelt and reach to the backseat to take our Chinese takeout.

"Are you going to scold them?" I ask giddish.

"You bet I am." She swings her door open but she doesn't stop out. "Before I go all psycho mode, I just wanted to tell you something."

I nod, motioning her to go ahead.

"I had fun today."

I pause for a second at her words. She had fun with me?

"I did too." Even though we could have done so much more, the boys actually weren't piss drunk and hungover, I loved the time I spent with Aria today. Making her laugh was my favorite part, more than anything else.

She's all smiles. When she's not all working up on something, she looks really beautiful. The way her smile is real and an inch longer. Her eyes are not burdened and her face glows. I like her more this way.

I really wanted to remove any worry from her life and keep her carefree.

A really weird thought to think about a girl who hasn't said that you both are friends? My brain chastises me.

"Let's go and blast some hung-over zombies." Aria cheers and I follow her suit.

We cross our lawn and I become really self-conscious about our grass. Aria is most probably used to seeing lush, green grass and I honestly don't remember the last time we mowed our lawn or even watered it.

My cheeks tint with embarrassment as I twist the key in the lock.

The door swings open and I take in the chaos reigning in the Corruption household.

Cade and Edwin are playing video games on the couch. I hear Andrew whining from the kitchen that there's no food in the house and slamming the fridge.

Edwin noticed the light glare on the TV and turned to me. "Hey man, how was today's session? Did you tell Ari—" His mouth opens as Aria steps in behind me. "—ahhhh. Aria! Hi."

Cade and Andrew look like they were caught in the kitchen at 2am.

"Hey, Aria. How are you?" They both pretend to be so chill but I knew them really well. They are scared shitless.

Her eyes narrowed into slits. "Good. Pretty good. I spent the last 4 hours making music with a band that lacked 3 of its 4 members." She slams the bags angrily on the counter. "You guys crashed my recording yesterday only to beg me that can I help you guys out. When I do agree, I don't see anyone in the studio except Callen."

"We had a reason." Andrew says slowly. I wanted to shake my head and do the *cut it out* sign to him. He's going to say something dumb and it was adding more alcohol to the already raging fire in Aria.

And as expected it flamed Aria even more. "Oh, please tell me what your reason was. I am on the edge of my seat."

"We were hung-over." He mumbles.

Aria looks at them in astonishment like she can't believe they called it a *'reason'*.

"Hung-over, my ass. You are playing video games." She gestures dramatically towards the TV. She did spot the third controller on the couch.

"It helps us with the headache."

Aria was ready to pounce on them. Her face was contorted in anger as she whips around to the counter and starts pulling boxes out of the cover and slamming them on the counter, mumbling angrily to herself.

Her happy demeanor that she had in the studio was gone and I weep at the disappearance of it.

"Oh, by the way, not only did I come around to see how serious you all are about being musicians, I also came to inform you that I was supposed to take your whole band on a writing retreat to LA."

"Whoa, that's really cool."

"It actually would have been cool." She agrees, nodding at the words. "If you were coming."

"What does that mean?" Edwin narrows his eyes in suspicion.

"It means that if you can't come to a writing session, what the hell would you do in a writing retreat?" She sorts out what she wants into one container and carries it to the sofa.

"Aria, it's not funny."

"Neither was not showing up to a session which I took out time from my schedule from. Also was throwing a party the night before."

Their shoulders slump in defeat.

"Callen and Cade will be coming with me though."

113

Cade's face fills with triumph and a bit of confusion. But Edwin is pissed with her decision.

"Why Cade? I understand why Callen is going but why Cade?"

"Because as much as he was at fault too, he's the songwriter in the group alongside Callen. We need him on the trip."

"This is so unfair."

"Don't talk about what's fair and what's unfair. I was supposed to be in my choreography practice at 10am but I canceled it for the writing session." Edwin opens his mouth to object but Aria holds a hand out to him. "No more discussion. Have food and take a few Advils. I don't want puking singers in the live room tomorrow."

They listen half willingly and go to the kitchen.

I take a seat beside Aria.

"Don't you think you were a bit harsh on them?"

"They will never learn. They are already 22. If they laze around, throw parties the night before important meetings, they will get a bad reputation. *Your* band will get a bad reputation."

"I know and I don't want that. I promise I will talk to them. But just go a little light on them when they do something stupid. They are new to this and they are my friends."

She nods, from the way her lips purse, she looks guilty and I don't want to make her feel that way.

"Is there no way we can take them?" I had no idea that Aria planned a writing retreat for us. To freaking LA. I was so grateful for what she was doing but leaving them here and taking only Cade with us when it's they're at equal fault doesn't seem like a fair decision.

"They won't be coming to LA with us." She says and before I could convince her, she continues. "They are going somewhere else."

"Somewhere else?"

"Andrew is going to Chicago and Edwin is going to London. I thought it would be good for them to learn better about what they like. If they see the world, they can bring a twist to the band." She admits. "I already texted Kate to book the tickets." She looks away with pink cheeks.

She's embarrassed that she always acts like a toughie, barking orders and being sassy. Believe me, she's all those things. But she's so much more than that. She has a heart of gold. I knew it the very second she helped me out in the middle of the road.

"You're such a softie, you know that?" I tease with a grin.

She acts highly offended. "I am not!"

"Yes, you are. Then why would you book a ticket for Andrew and Edwin to Chicago and London?"

"Wait, we're going too?" Edwin squeals from the doorway. He must have heard what I said. "Oh my god, Aria. You're the best!" He hops two feet above the ground in every step and throws his arm around Aria.

Meanwhile, she is glaring daggers at me. I leaked her little secret.

Oops.

Edwin runs off to tell the good news to Andrew.

"I hate you."

"Friends don't hate friends."

"Careful, Callen. Don't run off giving yourself that title." Something in her voice told me to run and grab that title.

"But aren't we friends?"

She gives it a thought. "Yeah, I guess."

"Exactly. You're just experiencing a moment of displeasure because I revealed that your heart is golden, not mechanical."

"I will kneel you in the balls."

"Friends don't kneel friends in the balls." I chastise her, laughing.

Before she could actually do any harm to me, an ear-splitting scream fills the living hall.

We turn our heads to the threat and it's 5 feet owl eyed, Olivia in Cade's T-shirt.

"OH MY GOD! I CAN'T BELIEVE IT! IT'S ARIA FROM THE CELESTIALS."

Aria's face drains of color, her spring roll half way to her mouth, when she realizes that this girl is most probably a fan and I burst into peals of laughter.

Chapter 20

ARIA

Callen's eyes are the size of saucers as he looks out of the window.

"I can't believe this."

"Did you ever think that you would come to LA? For writing your first album?"

"Not at all. I most probably would have gone to Minnesota and written about snow angels."

"That could be a good song."

He laughs, agreeing with it.

"I can come with you too." Olivia volunteers from Cade's arms.

I put a smile on my face, all bright and welcoming. Olivia is Cade's girlfriend. I met her two weeks ago at the boys house and could positively tell you that she talks. A lot.

But I get a feeling that this isn't her usual self. She looks like a friendly cool person but she always loses control of her mouth around me, blabbering god knows what.

I wish she somehow learns to calm herself down with me because since she's Cade's girlfriend, she's always going around.

Concert, studio and shooting, she will be there to support her boyfriend and I don't want her hyperactive, kid hyped on sugar self to be around at that time.

Nonetheless, she is a sweet girl and that might have been half of the reason that got her invited to LA. The other half was to get her to shut up.

Newsflash, it didn't work. She started screaming, louder after that.

"Ma'am, should I take you to a breakfast place?"

"Actually, it won't be necessary, Helsi. Drop us to the hotel, we will order room service there."

"Mr. Hayes insisted to have you breakfast."

"It's okay, Helsi. I will tell him that I ate at the hotel."

Helsi nods and pays undivided attention to driving.

"Who is Hayes?" Cade asks.

"He's our producer. Oh, even Chase will be here too."

"Nice. How long are we staying here?"

"How long do you want?" I answer, shrugging.

They look at me confused.

"You can stay how long you want. Writing retreat is basically writing your album. The whole process might last for 2 weeks, a month, two months. As long as you feel like you're done writing, we stay in LA."

"That's really cool. Hey, what about all the meetings we scheduled for us?"

"If it's really important, we normally video call. If it's something that doesn't need every member, then one person from the band attends. And if it's something not worth troubling the band over, the management handles it."

"Must be cool living like this."

"To a point, yeah." I say, distracted.

Callen is back to admiring the city with his curious brown eyes and they strike me in so deep. He gets so excited, looking at everything with wonder.

It's been so long since I felt that kind of excitement in me. Over anything, it's all black and white now, nothing more. The only time I saw color was when I played music.

It never occurred to me how much the world has changed for me when I listen to Callen's questions about the most random topics, his excited smile over things which most probably don't even deserve his precious fawning.

It's all black and white now
Colors have gone down the drain
I am looking at the sky
The sun isn't shining anymore
I live in a world where no one serenades the moon
Where did it all go wrong?

A knock on the door awakens me from my sleep.
I rub the sleep from my eyes as I stumble to the door.
Callen is standing on the other side of it.

Am I dreaming or does he actually look this good all time?

His hair was a tousled mess which would make a straightener cry but he somehow managed to pull it off. He had sweatpants on, *gray ones*, and an undershirt with a woolen jacket over his muscles which were teasing me.

You just woke up, Aria. Get a grip.

"Hey." My voice was rasp from sleep.

A smile tugs his lips and I try all my best not to look at it. Geez, someone woke up from the horny side today.

"Did I disturb you from your sleep?"

"No, the prince was supposed to come to wake me up anytime now." I motion him in and he steps in.

The faint smell of his deodorant tickles my nose as he passes by me.

I close the door, chastising myself to wake up from the lingering slumber. When I turn, I see Callen's eyes *lingering* at me.

Not my face but my bare legs.

I went to sleep in shorts. *Shoot.*

"I thought you would be awake." Callen comments, sitting down on my bed.

"And what is the reason for you to think that?" I ask, sitting on the other side on the bed, where I was sleeping.

"Because it's early morning."

"I don't believe you." It was still dark outside. I could clearly see it from the window.

Callen looks at me with a *really?* look.

I swipe my phone off the lamp table and tap it to light it up.

"2:30?" I gasped at the time. "It's 2:30 in the morning?"

"Yeah, it is. Not an ideal time to knock at a girl's door, I know but I thought you already had your fill of sleep and would be awake. I actually thought of going to Cade's room but I don't think I can. Their room is right next to mine. Headboards bang." He shakes his head.

"Wait, did I actually sleep for 14 hours?"

We had breakfast at 8 and went through all the studio bookings and meeting Hayes and Chase till afternoon. I was really tired so I went to bed at 12:15pm. And now, it's 2: 30 in the morning.

I slept for 14 hours straight and didn't even wake up once. Even for peeing.

"You look shocked."

"I have never slept this long. Not since I was 12."

"No wonder you look so relaxed and fresh. How long do you sleep on a daily basis?"

"Squeeze nap time whenever you can. Most to most 4-5 hours of sleep. It's a luxury when I get more than that."

"You're a human, Aria. Not a machine." He says disapprovingly.

I lie down on the fluffy pillows.

"I know." I whisper.

"You need sleep."

"I know."

"It's a basic necessity."

"Hmm."

"Next to eating the hotel's banana split."

I laugh a little. He cozies himself on the bed. "You seriously have to. It's the best I have ever had."

"That's what he said."

"Very mature of you. Back to the split. They are all synonyms of deliciousness."

"Let's order it then."

"Really?"

I dangle my legs down the bed as I reach for the receiver. "There is a reason why night staffs are hired, you know." I look over my shoulder at him and he makes a comical face at me. I continue with a smile.

The person picks up and I order two bananas split with extra walnuts because Callen wants them and we start talking.

"What should we do? Our studio session doesn't start till 9 in the morning."

"Who says we need a studio when we can make music with a guitar?" He gloats.

"Where's the guitar, genius?" I point out. Just because I am a singer doesn't mean I carry instruments wherever I go.

"Wait for a second, angel." He rushes out of the room happily and I am on my bed, under the covers with a perplexed look on my face.

Angel?

Before I have any time to dwell on it, he comes back to my room with a whole ass guitar.

"How did you smuggle that?" I ask, amused.

"In the big black suitcase you body-shamed. I mean, luggage comes in all shapes and sizes."

"How did that pass the security check?"

"Because flying with a world famous singer has its perks. Who in their right mind would carry a 30 kgs case for this? I stuffed it in the suitcase."

"For the fun of it?"

"Absolutely. Want to write some songs?"

"Gladly."

We spend the time writing songs, eating banana split and cracking jokes.

I laughed so hard at times which made Callen laugh harder and our stomachs were aching from laughing.

After almost 2 hours, we came up with a decent song called '*Late night banana splits*'.

It was a good way to commemorate our night together.

"This is a masterpiece." Callen says as soon as we finish singing it.

"Every song is a masterpiece for you."

"Every song written with you is." He winks and all the post thoughts after waking up came rushing back to me.

I think it's the first time he winked at me.

A brilliant idea pops in my head.

"Hey, we need to document this historic night." I leap off my bed.

"With someone more than a song?" He jokes as I rummage through my luggage.

Mental note: Put the clothes in the closet in the morning. Don't live like a hobo for the next few weeks.

"A picture." I present my camera grandly.

"Is that a Polaroid?"

"Yes, it is." I skip to his side.

We kept ourselves on two sides. He was in the cleanly made part of the bed and I was under the covers.

First, I didn't want my legs to be a centerpiece even they look amazing after I waxed and tanned them recently. And secondly, I call him a friend. But he feels like a friend who is so goddamn sexy that you want to rip the white undershirt off and wrap yourself around him, not his woolen jacket which was an inanimate clothing item I was envious of.

I position the camera above us so it covers us both and click a picture. The flash almost blinds my eyes, but at least I got the picture.

The Polaroid prints out and I keep it between the sheets to warm them up.

"Who knew? Aria Bastian is a polaroid girl." He teases.

"Smile." I sing out as I pan the lens at him. Callen gives me the most beautiful smile and I nearly melt into a puddle at the sight.

I press the button with a wobbly finger. The photo springs out and I again place it on the comforter.

"I find polaroid cute. It's way better than clicking pictures on a phone which you can easily delete." I say. "This." I picked up our picture. "Is permanent."

"That is a beautiful philosophy."

"I am full of them." I laugh at myself as I lie on my side, head supported by my elbow.

"I don't deny it." He lies on his side, mirroring my position. His eyes drift to the window and I steal the moment to look at his sculpted face.

Callen was art. You would look at him in awe, admire him in a room because no one else deserve the admiration than he did.

His face. Set of eyes so beautiful that you lose yourself in them. It's hard to fake things when you have brown eyes like his. He's everything and a little bit more.

"Hey, look." He points towards the windows and I follow his fingertips to see the color of the sky changing from black. It was becoming lighter.

"Sunrise." I mutter.

"Let's watch it!"

"Are you crazy? It's at least 2 degrees out there."

"Every sunrise is worth the frost bite, baby. Get up, let's watch it together." He springs out of the bed as if someone suddenly pumped life into him.

I open my mouth to object but he stops me. "I don't want to hear any excuses, Bastian. Get your warm ass up and onto the balcony."

"Warm ass?"

"Well, you're in a heated room."

"Stop thinking about the temperature of my ass, Cox."

He laughs, pulling me up with his strong hands and pushes me towards the balcony.

A chill of coldness spreads to my bare legs and I abort. "Too cold. Too cold."

"Don't move. I will get blankets."

I shiver in the cold as Callen finds the much needed blankets.

He comes outside and lays one down on the floor. I sit on it and my butt defrosts a little. Callen sits beside me and wraps another blanket around *us*. When I gave him a questioning look, "There were only two blankets, sorry."

He didn't sound that sorry.

I wanted to mind but I honestly didn't. We were wrapped in a fleece blanket and his body heat warmed me up so I wasn't complaining.

The sun shimmered in the LA skyline, bouncing its rays off glass buildings making a spectrum.

It was decorative and divine.

I let my head fall on Callen's shoulder. He stiffs up for a second before relaxing. I felt the tousled hair I liked so much before touching my head as he rested his head on mine.

Together, we watch the sunrise.

I close my eyes. Not only was the sunrise beautiful, what I was feeling was too.

It was gooey things, fireworks with a calm and safe feeling.

I don't think of the world. I don't think of my career, I don't think of all the things I have lost down the road. I think about this blanket and who I was with inside it.

I feel…happy.

Chapter 21

ARIA

"It looks like we are in Venice. This cafe is so pretty."
My weaknesses are pretty cafes.

The one I'm sitting in right now is white walled with
plant designs on them. Callen thought it would be a good
idea to sit on the tables outside and I couldn't agree more.
The weather was nice and cool and the food was
exceptional.

Cade and Olivia didn't join us for breakfast as they had
their own things to do. Headboards banging and all. Their
libido shocks me sometimes. It's been 3 weeks we are in
LA and they both shag, a lot.

But I didn't mind their absence even though Olivia has
learnt how to talk to me without shattering my eardrums.

I have been feeling so happy these days or whatever
gooey feeling I have in my chest. It was like a cloud
suspended into me and I was floating in it. No one could
even pull me down and I am away from all the worries.

"Have you been to Venice?" Callen asks me as he
takes a bite of his crepe.

"Twice. For Lexa's fashion show. It's a beautiful place. You should visit."

"Maybe after we are done recording the album." He agrees. "It's a bummer we are leaving today."

I wince at the reminder. "It is, isn't it?" This is the fastest I have ever written an album. Zeenat and I were shocked when we were finalizing the songs which we could record. We got 16 of them!

Normally it took at least 2 months to be done with writing but this time, it was different.

Callen and I made a great team. We experimented, made fresh tunes and beats. Cade said that even their band had more than enough songs for their album so it's a win-win for both of the bands.

I immediately felt tired. I don't want to go back home. I don't want to do interviews. I don't want to attend meetings. I wanted to stay here.

Callen suddenly brightens up. "Hey, if we are leaving this evening, we better make good use of our time, right?" He wiggles his eyebrows at me.

"We have an interview with Teen Pop in 3 hours." I reply sullenly.

"Then we make use of those 3 hours." He stands up, lending a hand to me. I stare up at him and he stares down at me. *"Please, Aria."*

I place my hand in his, biting down the smile I wanted to let out so bad.

He pays for the food and we leave the cafe. "So where would you like to go?"

Anywhere you take me.

"I don't have a specific place in mind." I say nonchalantly.

"What about the pier?"

"Pier?"

"Santa Monica Pier and beach. You have been to LA more than once right?"

I nod.

"Then why don't you know the pier? It's famous."

I am a bit embarrassed to admit it. I didn't care much about exploring the cities I have been in. In my free time, I catch up on sleep or spend time with the girls. "We normally don't get time to check out places."

"We are going there. Now. I can't believe that you didn't go to Santa Monica till now. Baywatch was filmed there."

I haven't seen that show yet.

"You haven't watched Baywatch, have you?" He whispers lowly like if he actually says out loud, people might hear us and boycott us for not watching that show.

I shake my head, mortified.

"I can't believe my best friend hasn't watched Baywatch and not gone to Santa Monica pier even though she has come to LA many times." He tears up like a drama queen.

I push him away, laughing. "Shut up, Cal."

We caught a cab to the pier. And when we reach there, he takes me directly to a cycling shop and rents two cycles.

"How do you know so much about this place?" I was curious.

"Google reviews and tourism websites. Gotta live one or another way." He shrugs.

We take our cycles out. He has a dashing purple one and my cycle was orange. "Please tell me you know how to ride a cycle or did you not get time for that too?"

"Ha. Ha. Ha." I mock him sarcastically. Cycling was a core memory. I obviously remember even if I haven't cycled in 6 years.

I'm a little wobbly at first. But then I remember Dad. His kind, supportive eyes guided me. *It's all about balancing and letting yourself free, Ryanne. I'm right behind you, holding you. Trust your Dad, I won't let you fall, my Ryanne.*

128

I gulp. Not his words, not now, not when I am with Callen. I want to be happy. Just for a little bit more.

"Look at you, you're a champ." Callen's cycle comes beside me.

"I told you so." I gloat.

We ride down the pier and I make sure not to crash into people or vendors. My hair was flying behind me and I was smiling. My legs ache but it's a sweet kind of pain. I close my eyes and think, I like living this life.

"For you, my lady." Callen gets us cotton candy. He hands me over two.

"Two for me?"

"Zeenat told me that you like cotton candy so I bought two for you."

I suppress a grin and I pull a bite out of it. One was blue cotton candy, another was pink.

"Freeze." Callen says suddenly.

"Yes?"

He whips out his phone and clicks a picture of me, then looks at me sheepishly. "You looked really cute and the sun angled perfectly on your face." He explains, tucking his phone in.

Redness spreads my cheeks at his compliment. It's not like I was the only one affected by it. I see his neck pink too as he walks in front of me.

"Hey, wanna ride the Ferris Wheel?"

I check the time. Exactly 30 minutes. Then I leave for the interview and we directly meet at the airport for the flight back home. I wanted to say no and bow out from the Ferris riding request. I could do something more useful than sit in a circling ride. But my heart didn't agree with me. I wanted to see what the world looked like from above.

"Sure."

A satisfactory glow illuminates Callen's face in the afternoon sun. "My girl is quite a daredevil." He winks.

129

And my heart flutters its beat. *There he goes again, winking at me like it won't give me a cardiac arrest.*

He extends his hand again to me and I place it in his, without any doubt, without any hesitation.

We got the ticket to Ferris Wheel and the people in the line were eyeing me differently. I inch a bit closer to Callen. I don't know why but the crowd were wearing a perplexed and curious expression on their faces.

The man in-charge there starts letting everyone in on their seats. When we are the next in line, I feel a tap on my thigh.

I look down and immediately smile as I see a cute pigtailed girl.

"Hey there."

"Hi." She says swaying in her cute frock. "Are you the one who sang Daisies on the moon?"

I pout at her cuteness. She was adorable with her flower frock, blond pigtails and a soft stuffed bunny in her hand.

I bend to her teeny height.

"Yes, I am. But can we keep it a secret?"

"Okay. Can you please sign my Bow Bow for me?"

"Sure, sweetie." I always carry a pen in my bag because you never know when you will need it. Lexa used to make fun of me and called me too Mommy-like. But it's worth it when you sign little kids stuffed bunnies.

I sign my name and give many hearts and kisses on the back of the bunny.

"What's your name, honey?" I ask as I make a heart.

"Calliope." She giggles as if her name is the funniest thing she has ever said.

My smile drops suddenly at the name.

"That's a really beautiful name."

She's all smiles again. "Thank you."

"Go to your mommy. She might be worried about you. It was nice meeting you, Calliope." I caress her cheek. Saying the name also hurts. "You too, Bow Bow."

She laughs, a radiant carefree laugh and waves bye to me as she goes back into the crowd. I hope she finds her mother.

I stand up, dusting my jeans and I find Callen staring at me, with something I don't recognize. "You're really great with kids."

"Only the good ones." I point out, giving out a laugh I didn't feel.

As we stepped into our carriage, I heard a little girl's voice squeal. "Mommy, I met the girl who sang Daisies on the moon!"

And the whole crowd goes wild.

Chapter 22

CALLEN

"Good night." I raise my hand in parting with Cade and he yawns in return.

"Good night to you too. Don't you dare come and wake me up, asking for breakfast." He warns before entering his apartment.

I smile at his warning. He clearly knows that none of us will listen to it. Edwin and Andrew arrive tomorrow morning. For sure they will wake him up, demanding breakfast.

I unlocked the door to my apartment and it was home sweet home. I have been living in this home for only 3 months and this is the only place after my parents' house that I ever felt like home.

After several hours of driving, I was tired and ready for bed. But my suitcase mocked me from the entrance.

I remember Aria coming to my room from something back in LA. It had been a week staying there. She gasped in pure horror when she saw that I was still taking clothes out of my suitcase. She scolded me to not live like a hobo and told me to put my clothes in the closet right that instant.

Somehow, my suitcase developed an evil sense and nagged me to put my clothes in the closet before sleeping.

"Asshole suitcases." I mutter, yanking them to my room.

As I shelf my clothes, my mind wanders back to LA and the days there. It doesn't take a long time to figure out that Aria was in many.

I had so much fun with her. Aria was a girl who had it all but she couldn't enjoy any because she was always working for more.

I don't think she wants more and more money. It feels like she forgot how to live, be happy and enjoy life. Even if for once.

I saw the light in her spark again when I wanted her to come with me to breakfast places, in the balcony with our favorite desserts, the pier. I am pretty sure we increased a pound or two but it doesn't matter.

A life isn't worth living if you don't actually live it.

What strike me the most was the Ferris Wheel. When the girl said her name as Calliope. For some reason, Aria's face went colorless as if she saw a ghost. It wouldn't take a detective to figure out that Calliope was a name that terrorized her. If the word was repeated again, she would cry and wither in pain.

We sat in the carriage right in time before the little girl told her mom that Aria is the singer of *Daisies On The Moon*. It didn't take anyone more than a split second to figure it out and Aria's cover blew faster than dandelions in the wind.

We called her personal security because the crowd was going crazy on the ground while we were feet above them in the air.

With the tension of fans below and the name, Calliope, Aria's mood fouled completely. She didn't talk to me till we reached the hotel. She apologized for whatever happened and left to go to her room.

After that, I saw her in the airport and it looked like things took a turn for the worst. Olivia tried talking to her but she was in a completely different headspace. Lexa flew in too. Her flight was supposed to be back home tomorrow with Edwin but for some reason, she came to LA. Ver went to her boyfriend's parents' house so she wasn't there. I bet that if she didn't have family obligations, even she would be hopping the first flight to LA.

Nor Zeenat or Lexa left Aria's side for even one second till we landed back home.

We had cars to take us back home. They were loading the luggage into the car when Aria came to me. She said, "I had fun on this trip. Thank you, Callen."

I swear I could see the tears threatening to leave her eyes. I wanted to hug her at that right moment and make all her pain go away. I want to fight every demon in her head and every monster in her closet so she doesn't have to fight it anymore.

Aria turned, leaving and I was standing there with words I couldn't speak.

I finish arranging my clothes in the closet and lie down on my bed.

Sleep clouds me and I keep thinking about the same question over and over again.

Who is Aria's monster?

Chapter 23

CALLEN

"She's a great photographer, don't you worry. Everyone loves her work. Actually, you guys have to be great for *her*." Pierre cackles.

Edwin and I exchange a look.

"Thank you so much, Pierre, for your *advice*." Cade pats Pierre and pushes him out of the door like a friendly and gentle way an annoyed person would do.

French people always fascinated me. I love their culture, their food and places of attraction. The people are very friendly too. As much as I have heard, Pierre is the opposite of them. He talks in a high pitched and nasally as possible. Most of his time he does talk, it's just to insult us.

I don't even think he is French. Maybe a mix of many ancestors of different countries. Only his name and hint of accent gives away that he *might* be French.

The door opens again and it's Sandra. My body immediately relaxes. Thank god it's not another burst of Pierre.

Sandra was our personal assistant. She contacted us about your schedules and meetings for that day. She made sure we had transport ready and that everything was up to date.

What made her even better was that she was our mom's age, not a young PA. The boys wanted a hot shot young lady, Andrew especially, but what if you like the girl and she likes you? Disaster waiting to be unfolded.

Like I say. Never mix business and like, love or lust or any kind of L to be honest, together.

"She's ready for you." Sandra nods at us.

We nod, fixing any hair that strands that decided to go rogue and check outfits once again.

"Who do you think it is?" Andrew asks, coming beside me.

"I have no idea. I think we will find out soon enough."

And we did. A woman with drop dead gorgeous curves had her back towards us, talking to Pierre. As if she heard us, her long black hair swished in the air as she turned around.

"Hey, Ms. Photographer!" Andrew goes to hug her and then stops suddenly, remembering she doesn't hug and ends up putting his hand on her shoulder, greeting her.

"Oh my god, Callen. It's *Aria*. Our photographer is *Aria*. Can you believe it's *Aria*?" He and Aria have been getting along very well nowadays. They even went shopping a few days before.

"I can totally believe it." I mutter, looking at her as she talks to Cade and Andrew. They say something and she laughs. I notice the difference in her laugh better than anyone else. It lacked life. And neither did it light up her eyes.

Edwin skips to Aria as if he is frolicking through a field and they do a weird greeting where they wiggle their fingers at each other with the goofiest grin on their face.

"And I kept on telling Callen that we should order from the ramen place but Mr. Big shot here," Aria's eyes snap to me at the mention of my name and they stay there. She occasionally nods and tries to look interested in Andrew's story but till the end, I was fixated on her and she was on me.

Something was definitely up with her. She didn't seem her usual self. The look in her eyes. They were unreadable. Normally, she is tense or shouting on someone but now, her shoulders hang low and her chin lower.

Worry fills me. *Has she been eating and sleeping properly? What was troubling her so much?*

Aria claps her hand, bringing everyone's attention to her.

"Hi everyone! I am happy to be working with all of you today. This is the band we will be shooting today, Corruption." The team starts clapping, welcoming us. "I would like you to be patient with them. It's their first photo-shoot." They all give an understanding nod. "Let's get to business, people."

Aria does a few test runs with lighting and camera and then assigns us places to sit on the white backdrop.

She clicks a few photos, the flash burns into my retinas, making my eyes water. On the pause, I rubbed my eyes. I hear footsteps approaching me. I look from one eye open to Aria in front of me.

She bends to my face level and dust my eyes off, her soft finger brushing my eyelids. Then she fixes my posture and angle. When I feel the slight twitch in her fingers as she touches me, I know it's not going to be an easy night.

Cade's individual shot wraps up.
"Do I look hot?" He asks.

137

"Why don't I send it to Olivia and let her be a judge of it?" Aria says. They both check shots of Cade and he looks satisfied.

My phone pings with another message from the sibling's text group. Cameron was telling us about his 'hot' hookup.

Cameron- *That's how it ended.*
Missy- *What do you need? A applause for it?*
Cameron- *Don't worry. The girl applauded me after we were done.*
Missy- *Golden star for you, Cam.*

I could hear Missy saying it sarcastically in my head.

Missy- *I don't even believe that any guy would be good in sex. You just insert it in and out. That's it. What is your accomplishment?*
Cameron- *Sex is more than in & out. But what will your single status on Facebook know about it?*
Missy- *First of all, who uses Facebook anymore? Second on the agenda, I can get a boy to fall head over heels in love with me till next month's family dinner. Want to bet?*
Cameron- *God, please no. We are completely happy and at peace with you not dating anyone. Right, Callen?*
Callen- *Right.*
Missy- *Guitar boy sounds distracted…*
Cameron- *Most probably he is staring at his prissy, perfect girlfriend*
Callen- *Who is she? Pray tell, me, who is this secretive girl I myself know nothing about*
Cameron- *Ms. Aria Bastian. Smoking a hot body. Ass and voice sent by god. She's something else.*
Missy- *Would you please stop objectifying a dignified woman for one second?*
Callen- *Exactly, Cam. Shut up.*

Cameron- Stop attacking your poor bro for some girl, man.

Callen- She's not some girl, she's my friend. Don't speak about her like that. I don't like it.

Cameron- sorry, bro.

Missy- damnnn. Callen is protective of his girl.

Callen- I am not.

Cameron- Clear lie

Missy- Crystal clear. C'mon, Cal. I know you are feeling something for her.

Callen- Nothing but friendship.

Missy- Bad liar. This reminds me of a Selena Gomez song.

Callen- Don't sing it!

Cameron- Don't sing it!

Missy- Jesus, people.

"Callen, you coming?"

I raise my head and I see Aria's expectant eyes looking back at me.

"Huh?"

"You coming? For the solo photos?"

"Where's Cade?"

"He left just a minute ago. Didn't you hear him say goodbye to you?"

"Umm, no."

Shit. Edwin and Andrew already left after their solo shots to the nearest bar. Cade most probably went there too.

"I'm sorry. I will be there."

I quickly text a goodbye to my siblings and slip on my plaid jacket.

"Ready?" Aria asks as I settle on the chair.

"Yes." I replied. Leaning forward on my elbows, I look at the camera.

She squats, positioning the camera on her face.

I take the moment to take her in properly. She straightened her hair today. The perfection of her hair was applaudable. Not even one strand out of its place, not a single split end. Straight black hair that flowed behind her like a curtain.

She wore a black turtleneck and fitted pants. Cameron wasn't lying when he told those things about her.

The tension between us is palpable and I want to break the ice but I don't know how.

The flash goes off as the first photo is clicked.

Chapter 24

ARIA

He looks anxious.

He's fidgeting, darting his eyes here and there. Unable to contain himself.

I couldn't help but think I'm the reason he is acting this way.

There was too much darkness in me, too many unopened doors and unresolved issues. I starved off people's happiness and light. *I was a pest.*

I practiced a lot to put on the face I wore every day. The smile was fake but feels real after being this way for far too long. I practice smiling 100 smiles in the mirror every day. Making sure I don't slip up in front of anyone.

Every day was a play and I was the lead actress, acting my way around it.

Out of all the people I met, known and spoken to, Callen scares me the most. He is opposite to what I am.

Genuine, real, happy and adventurous. He's all that. And he is trying to figure me out. Not the fake Aria, the real one. He has reached my walls, searching a way in through the perimeter.

What scared me the most is that he might actually find a way in.

"Lie down."

He doesn't even question what I asked him to do. He keeps the chair aside and surrenders himself on the white spotless ground.

I liked taking pictures from above. When they are down, they are completely defenseless and vulnerable. That's what makes the best picture. Vulnerability is beautiful.

I clicked a picture of him. He looks beautiful in real life and is possessing in a camera lens.

Something unexpected happens. His fingertips skim my ankles. The touch was feather light. If I wasn't so aware of my body around him, I wouldn't even have felt it.

He again swipes his fingertips along the little exposed skin. I was wearing a black turtleneck, full sleeves, and pants reaching all the way down. Everything was covered in cloth and shoes except my ankle.

"You look beautiful." Callen whispers and I feel like I could explode from the compliment.

I gulp, bending down on my hips to take a closer shot of him.

His eyes bore into the camera and it almost felt like he could see what I was seeing, listening to what I was thinking, feeling what I was feeling.

The camera clicks and the sound of echoes as the flash goes off.

Callen's hands start to rise upwards from my ankle. My leg shivers slightly on his touch. He is maintaining eye contact with me and is taking me out of my senses.

They reach right behind my knees and rest there. Before I could say something to him, he yanks me and I lose my balance falling right on top of him.

"Callen!" I gasp in surprise.

"What is it, Angel?" He asks, getting up, placing his hands on my hips. "Do I make you nervous, baby?"

He suddenly switches our position. He is on top of me and I am sprawled over the floor. Vulnerable and defenseless.

"Or does this scare you?" He motions his chin between the tight space between us. Even in a horizontal position, he towers me. Callen pushes the bangs that have fallen on my eyes.

"This." I whisper, honestly. This scares me. Me and Callen. We haven't started yet. There are ways this might go right but so many ways it can go wrong too.

"Why?"

I bite my lips. I wanted to scream that I didn't know. I have never been so conflicted yet feel so alive at the same time.

Callen plucks the forgotten camera from my pale white hands and holds it up to his face.

He is clicking a picture of me.

"Are you afraid of what we will become?" I don't answer, just look at him. He clicks a picture.

"Are you afraid that you won't be into this relationship as much as I would be?"

"Impossible."

He doesn't click a photo when I answer.

"Do you like me?"

"You're not that annoying."

Callen smiles.

"Do you like me being around you?"

I nod.

His smile couldn't get any wider but it did.

"Then why are you ignoring me?"

"Because I'm guilty." It flows out of my mouth. The barrier was gone around him. He was pulling answers out of me.

"For?" He presses. My lips seal for further explanation.

He gets that I'm not going to say anything about it, he nods to himself.

"Who's Calliope?"

The name draws daggers to my heart, ripping my barely living heart apart.

A pained, shudder breath slips out of my mouth. Callen rests one of his hands at the side of my head.

"Did she hurt you, Aria?"

"She's no one."

She was my everything. The sun in my sky. The beautiful moon that lit up my night. The reason why I was here.

Now even the name of her rips me to shreds, weeping on the floor.

Tears flow down my face as I look at Callen's hovering face.

"She wasn't anyone. She was the whole world for you, wasn't she?"

The pain in my heart intensifies. I can feel it, taking over my chest.

"You're hurting, baby." He caresses my cheek, looking down at me in sadness.

I am. It's hurting so bad, Callen. So bad.

Help me.

"Talk to me."

My sobs turn harder. Nothing seems nice now. The blackness was right around the corner.

"Leave me." I don't know if he can hear me or did I say it in my head?

"What?"

"I said." I gather more power into my voice. "Leave!"

I push on his chest hard.

He doesn't bulge at my push.

"Aria…"

"Get out. I don't want to be near you."

He opens his mouth again but I push again.

"Go away!" My throat is raw from screaming.

144

He tries to talk to me again but I turn my head the other side.

He finally gets up. I can feel him linger. But he eventually leaves and with that, I let out the trapped cries in my throat. Ugly memories evade me and I doubled over, crying hard.

Mama and Astra's happiest memories replay in my mind for the thousandth time. Once upon a time, they were happy memories, now they bring me pain to cripple me away.

I always hoped I died this way, repenting for my sins, drenched in sweat and tears, praying to god to take me because I didn't want to live here anymore.

I lie on the cold linoleum floor, sob racking one after another, alone and lonely.

This would be a good way to go.

Chapter 25

CALLEN

We don't talk for the next 2 weeks. All we had was utter silence, unspoken words and inexhaustible feelings.

I didn't want to unravel her. What I did that night haunted me every second of the day. Her wailing sobs. Her deep scared eyes like she is barely holding on to the rope and she might slip any second, falling into an abyss.

During the duration of two weeks, we had our video shoot. For our new song with Celestials. They produced it with Hayes, Chase and a man called Sergio directed it. He did look a lot like the Professor from Money Heist.

Aria and I had a scene together. When we were done taking it, I didn't even hang back to see the final product and ran to the dressing room, feeling that my body was on fire. I couldn't breathe beside her. She zapped the air away from my lungs.

But with the adoration that filled my heart with every time she gives a fantastic shot for the director. The way she looks confidently at the camera, lips sync the lyrics like she is the only one in the world who has the right to sing them.

That night.

I couldn't remove it out of my head. No matter how much I distract myself, I hear her sobs. I didn't leave the studio when she asked me to. I stayed behind. Right out of the door, staring at the strong woman I have known to crumble at the mention of a *name*. She drove off 10 minutes later after kicking me out of the studio.

She broke, she cried, she picked up her pieces and she left.

I hated myself for what I did to her. She was not feeling well, she was upset. All I did was push her off the cliff she was already dangling on.

I never redeemed myself as a bad person but now, I feel like the most horrible one on this earth.

Righting a wrong is what makes us human again. And I am going to beg, grovel and ask Aria for forgiveness like it's my last day on earth because if she doesn't forgive me, it might as well be.

I knock at the door. She knows I'm here because her security at the front gate told her. I half expected her to turn me away from there itself.

But she didn't.

The door opens and there is she. Standing in all her glory.

My chest was on fire at her sight. "Hey." I whisper. I didn't mean to whisper, I was dazed.

"Hi." Indifference coated her voice but not enough. She was acting. Acting again. Her eyes darted over my body, taking in the formal pants and black shirt. "Why did you come here?"

"To express a gesture."

"A gesture?"

"Yes. Can I come in?"

She assesses me with her eyes. Maybe she turns me away from here. At least I got past level 1. But I keep trying till I reach the last level, her heart.

Aria pushes the door open wider and a sigh of relief leaves my mouth.

She raises her eyebrows at me and I shake my head, smiling and enter inside.

The first thing I noticed about the house is that it's quiet.

"Where is everyone?"

"Out." Her clipped response comes with the shut of the door.

"You're alone?"

"I was hoping for it." She sizes me up and down before walking past me to the couch. She has a laptop sprawled over the carpet with a number of CDs.

I sit beside her on the carpet. From the glow of the laptop, I can see it's a video paused. Beside her were crumpled up tissues.

"What are you watching?"

This time, Aria doesn't look at me with cold contempt. There is fondness in her eyes as she answers me. "A visit down the memory lane."

"Can I see it with you?"

She hesitates.

"Please." I plead, trying to help my case.

"Okay." She puts the laptop on one of our legs each, balancing it between us and hits the play button.

A video starts playing. It is an old film. The one people used to record in their camcorders in the early 2000's. The video of a young woman with blonde hair and strawberry dress on. She is squatting on the ground, hands reached out. Giggling sounds coming from a source I couldn't see. Finally a little girl, very little, runs into her arms.

The girl strikes familiarity. Her hair texture, her nose and her eyes. Absolutely the same.

I look at Aria in surprise. A small smile tugs her lips.

"Don't be surprised. I was a kid once too."

"A very cute kid."

The young woman, who was most probably her mother, takes her and twirls her in her arms. Shrieks of laughter spill out of Toddler Aria as her mother spins her.

"Mommy, mommy! What about me?" Someone whines off camera. The person who is recording Aria and her mother turns to the voice and it's another kid.

She's wearing a white summer dress with a blue bunny pin in her hair.

She resembled Aria's mother more than Aria did herself with her blonde hair.

"You too, sweetie." She says *sweetie* the same way Aria says *sweetie*. Adorable and filled with affection.

The older girl runs to her mom. Other toddlers her age would have thrown a hissy fit but Aria doesn't mind sharing her mom.

Aria's brown eyes turn to the camera. "Daddy, can we get cotton candy?" She babbles in her still developing syllables.

"Sure, princess." A deep, kind voice says behind the camcorder and Aria's face lights up like a thousand suns.

"Why don't you give me the camcorder and take our little peanuts to get cotton candy?" The mother says to the camera man, the Dad.

I was assuming everyone's relation to Aria in this. I have no idea if the other little girl is actually her sister. She did call the women and man, mommy and daddy though.

The video turns from the woman and her kids to a huge, hefty man.

"C'mon, princesses." He extends his hands to his kids and they happily grab on.

149

Aria and her sister look like small toothpicks in front of their dad. Their tiny hands wrap around his big finger.

There is an cotton candy stall near them. The Dad turns to the camera.

"What color would you like, Calli?"

"Bubblegum, sweetie."

The next 3 minutes, they eat cotton candy and talk about grass and birds but my mind is stuck on one thing. What The Dad called The Mom.

Calli.

The video ends with pin-drop silence.

My mind is jumbling with questions.

"Calliope is my mother's name. Calliope Denver." Aria clears the air for me.

"Is she..." I didn't want to complete the sentence because I was scared that the worst thing to ever happen came true.

"Not there anymore."

Oh shit.

"Astra too. They met with an accident when I was 17."

"Aria." I didn't know what else to say. Guilt filled me.

This was her monster. The death of her mother and sister. This is why the name of Calliope darkened her. Because she didn't have a mother anymore. She didn't have a sister anymore. She was the last one standing.

"Don't pity me, Callen. I told it to you so you can quit pestering me about it."

"I wasn't trying to."

"Well, it looked a lot like it." She laughs bitterly.

"Aria, I didn't mean to intrude on your personal matters but you were really upset when after LA. I was worried about you."

"Why?"

"The truth?"

"Never lie." Vulnerability was heavy in her voice.

"Because you're my best friend and it hurts me to see you sad."

150

"I'm your best friend?"

"You are." My eyes soften.

"I never had a best friend before."

"What about your band? Lexa, Ver and Zeenat?"

"They are my sisters." Love tints her sentence.

"I never had a best friend before too. Maybe that's why we met each other, don't you think?"

"You think our meeting was fate?" She quirks her eyebrows at me.

"I do. How else are we so good together?" I say, convinced.

Aria laughs a little. It sounds weak. But I don't mind, it is a laugh. Something is always better than nothing.

"I like you, Callen."

"Took you long enough to admit it." I joke.

Her hair is not combed and stray strands hang loose.

I tuck them behind her ear. A small smile tugs my lip as she closes her eyes at the touch, leaning into it.

"You're hungry?" I ask her before I do something that wasn't in the plan. Tonight was about forgiveness, not thinking of how her lips would taste.

"A little."

"You want me to cook something?"

Her eyes fly open. "You know how to cook?"

"I do and today I'm going to make something for you." I grab her up.

"We can order something." She suggests.

"Blasphemy. I will be cooking for you."

"Is it necessary?"

"Absolutely."

I only learned how to cook basic stuff. My mom thought her kids well enough so they don't starve to death.

I planned to make spaghetti for dinner and Aria suggested making garlic bread. She seasoned the baguette pieces with garlic butter. As she bent over to keep the tray in the oven, I averted my eyes. I wasn't going to drool over her when she was vulnerable with me a few minutes ago. I was a man but I wasn't an idiot.

Aria leans her back on the counter, fixating her eyes on me. "Thank you."

"For?"

"For making dinner." She gestures to the simmering pasta sauce I was mixing. "And being here tonight."

"Sorry."

"For?"

"Being an idiot."

"I think I can live with that." She gives me a last precious smile and goes to the fridge to rummage something from inside.

"Honey, I'm home!" Someone shouts from the front door.

Aria's head pokes up from the fridge with a *what-the-hell?* look.

Ver enters the kitchen, all smiles. She doesn't spot me yet; her eyes are on Aria's tensed face.

"What are you doing back so early?"

"Before you go all ballistic on me, I have a very good reason to come back home. At 10pm."

Aria straightens, closing the fridge door. She has a champagne bottle in her hand.

"Oh, how did you know that we were celebrating?" Ver asks, plucking the bottle from her hands.

"I didn't." Aria mutters, her cheeks turning red. She glances at me and Ver turns at the flick of the eye contact and her jaw drops at me.

"Callen?" Calling her shocked would be an understatement. "Were you guys on a date or something?"

"NO!" We speak at the same time. Aria raises her eyebrows at me but I shrug. She had the same answer as me.

"That sounded forceful." Ver smirks with a cheeky smile.

"Get lost, V." Aria flicks Ver's forehead.

152

"Only for a while. I will change and come and then I will tell you the good news." Ver shimmies in her dress. "I'm all soaked and dirty."

"Do I want to know?" Aria asks. She takes her place on the counter beside me.

"You might not want to know but I'm going to tell you anyway." Ver gives us a flying kiss and runs up the stairs.

Aria smiles, shaking her head but then she looks at me and her smile drops with a sneer. "Why did you sound so highly offended when she asked us if we are on a date?"

"Hey, your reply was not so different from mine."

"So just the idea of going on a date with me is so unappetizing for you, right?"

I push the wooden ladle in her direction with pasta sauce on it. "Taste."

"Screw you."

"Please."

She reluctantly tastes it. Her tongue sloshes in her mouth as she takes in the flavor. She likes it. "Saying please doesn't get you things in the world."

"But it got you to taste the pasta sauce. I am a victorious man." I set the ladle and lower the heat on the pasta sauce. I have to add spaghetti in a while but I had something more important to do.

Aria takes me in with her eyes as I cover the short distance between us. My body towers over her. She's shorter than me but she isn't short. She emits fire and confidence.

"I wasn't offended that Ver asked if we were on a date. I was called out of what I really want." I keep a hand on the upper cabinet, entrapping her here within me. "The idea of going on a date with you is far from unappetizing. It's alluring. Just like you. I think about it every day. How I want to take you on a date. Hold your hand. Buy you flowers. Tell you how beautiful you look. Stare at you when you aren't looking."

153

She wasn't in a place where she could be in a relationship. And even if she does get into one, she won't expect commitment but a lifetime is what I want to promise her.

"I know, angel. You're not ready for a relationship right now. But I will wait for the day you kiss me. I can be a patient man when it comes to you even though I don't promise that when you become my girlfriend."

"I don't think you will last that long." She teases, the tension in her shoulder relaxing.

I don't even think I will last. Staying away from Aria is hell and heaven mixed in one.

"I promise you, I will make you happy. I will remove all your worries."

"Why?"

I cup her face, kissing her forehead. "Because you have been fighting too hard and for too long. I am here for you only, angel. And I will make it my living purpose to make you as happy as you deserve to be."

Chapter 26

ARIA

"I like that riff. It's classy and rebellious at the same time."

"That's exactly what I was going for." Zeenat grins.

"Off the sound board, you two. Lunch is here." Lexa announces, throwing the doors open, followed by Ver who was holding drinks.

For the life of me I couldn't make Lexa stop kicking down our doors. She felt like an assassin with Tom Cruise and I replaced 4 doors because of the dents she has put on them.

She grins at my disapproving look. There's a limit to correcting someone's annoying trait. If they don't listen, it's better to stop wasting your energy on them than sounding like a broken record.

"Hey, by the way, Niya called." Ver sets our drinks on the floorboard of our home studio.

"Oh really? Anything important?" I click around, saving all the songs we have worked on the computer.

"They have decided the tour dates."

All 3 of our heads turn at the same time towards her.

"Actually?"

"Actually." Ver nods at Lexa.

My heart keeps praying one thing over and over again. *Please let it not be this month. Please let it not be this month.*

6 months haven't been completed till now. I promised Ver and my band that I will give them 6 months off any concerts and I really wanted to keep my word. I did tell Niya about this too, hoping that my transparency with her got me some much needed humanity.

"Next month is the tour."

Yes! Fucking yes!

"And we know who we should thank for our 6 months off. Right?" Ver claps her hand in front of her and looks at me cheekily.

"Thank you, Aria." They all say unison like kids in a class and I laugh.

"It's our united efforts, girls. We deserve a month for us."

Our band had a distinct feature in us. We were quick in our work. Even if one of us has a writer block or couldn't get the dance steps right, the other always coaxes them out of it or into it.

I very well knew that we don't need 6 months of break from tour for writing an album. We would have done it while touring too.

But we were human beings after all. We needed the relaxation that no one ever gave to us so we lied to the management that it would take 6 months for us to finish the album and as they obviously couldn't lose their money making girl band, they agreed to give us how much time we want.

"One more month. That's nice." Zeenat acknowledges as we eat.

"Good thing we got time to start up on this one's wedding." I nudge Ver with my foot and she lights up again.

She has loved weddings since she was a kid. I experienced it with her first hand being her friend. Now that Cash finally popped the question and a diamond ring, she is floating on cloud 9. They are planning to get married at the end of this year. After the tour and launch of our new album. Our fans would go crazy, we have so much in store for them for the next 7 months.

"You still need to decide who is your maid of honor." Lexa points out and Ver's face pales at the question.

Another thing we love doing is asking who is going to be her maid of honor. We don't even mind who she chooses. Either as a maid of honor or bridesmaid, we will be there on her special day no matter what.

The ranking in a wedding doesn't matter when it's her wedding. Ver is a sister to me. We don't have the same DNA but she has always held my hands through the ups, downs and rock bottom, cloud 9.

"Guys, don't do this to me." She pleads.

"Cmon huns, don't pressurize her." Lexa shushes it down. "Everyone knows that she will choose me."

We throw ketchup packets on her.

"Hey, I am going to be the best option for it. There are some facts we can't fight. It's universal."

That gets her the extra spoons on her face.

"You guys are just jealous." She sticks her tongue at us.

"And you're just delusional." I wiggle my spoon in the air.

"Delusional is telling you that nothing is going on between you and Callen." Lexa shoots back.

"For the love of everything holy, nothing is going on between us. We're just friends."

Even after the promise he took.

"I was a witness." Ver raises her hand. "Of something hot." She teases.

"Man, shut up."

"Ms. Bastian is getting aggressive. Better call the witness protection program. Ver is not safe anymore." Zeenat flares dramatically.

"Let me clear it out once in and for all, me and Callen are just friends. *For the time being anyways.*"

Lexa catches it within a fraction of second. "Time being? *TIME BEING?*" She shouts.

I purse my lips, not wanting to say anything but some things are definite in this world and one of them is even if I don't want to tell, they will pry it out of me.

I tell them from the unexpected visit of Callen at the door step to disclosing about what happened to Mom and Astra to him making dinner for me till the promise he took.

He is letting me take the reign and is blindly riding this metaphorical horse that is our relationship off the cliff with me. The amount of trust he puts on me scares me sometimes.

"And you told us nothing is going on between you both. Friends don't make promises of taking their friends on a date and kissing them." Lexa says. She seemed way too happy about what I just said but I don't feel the same way

"You don't want to give him a chance, do you?" Zeenat reads the tension on my face.

I gulp, my face dropping even more.

"Baby, why?" Ver asks, huddling closer to me.

"Because I'm a mess." I break down. No warning, no stimuli. "It's been 4 years since Mama and Astra died. I haven't spoken to Dad till now. I don't even know where the hell he is. He was the remaining family I had and I kicked him to the curb. I heard Mom's name from a little girl and it felt like a black hole opened behind me and a hand reached out, grabbing me and pulling me into the hole. Ever since then, I am in my worst mental state. I can't sleep properly. I am having nightmares again and if even once my mind is not occupied by work then the image of their dead bodies play again and again till I feel like I'm going to explode. When I am going to fight with myself every day, trying to prove that I'm still fine, how can I go and start dating someone else? Dating requires commitment, love, care, and attention. I can't give it to him when I don't have it in me. I'm fucking made of *steel*." Till I finish talking, I'm a tearful mess.

Ver, Lexa and Zeenat huddle me and I cry into their familiar arms. They were always there to help me, pick me from the lows or to just cry on.

"Ari, we love you. If you feel like you don't want to get into a relationship, we understand." Lexa kisses my forehead.

I nod, wiping my tears away. I lost my cool. At least I lost in front of the girls more than someone else.

"It's not like I don't like him. I like him so much." His bright smile, his understanding nods. He pulls me out of my daily routine to just let me feel the adrenaline of living. Small touches he takes on me and still convinces me that we are friends and *his promise*. "He's such a pure soul. I don't want to break his heart."

"You won't." Zeenat says with enough conviction that I wanted to laugh.

We wrap up the crying fest and do vocal warm ups for the song we are about to record. Ver and I are picking up the empty containers off the ground.

"Can I tell you something?" Ver asks.

"Hmm, sure."

"Before I say anything, I am not a love expert but a few years of dating gives you a bit of knowledge in that department."

I smile.

"Cash didn't have the most supportive parents, career wise. They didn't like their teen son dying his hair, singing profanities and wearing fancy coats without shirts underneath. Totally understandable if you see it from the eyes of a 90's parent. Right?" She tossed plastic forks into

159

the bag. "Cash struggled a lot. I think he was a people pleaser since he was a kid but that need intensified when he became a rapper."

I used to get a hint of that when I met him for the first time in high school. He said he liked meat even though he was a vegetarian. He also likes sky gliding but when Lexa said that she is afraid of heights, he backtracked.

Ver rubs her neck as if she's embarrassed of what she's doing to say next. "He did a lot of things that he wasn't supposed to. Took a few injections, tried to change his vocal chords so he could get people to like him. He abused drugs and liquor."

I remember that time too. Ver got a call from the hospital and started crying. As she wasn't in the state of driving herself to the hospital, I took her there and when she rushed to the reception, I saw nothing but fear in her face. She was scared to lose Cash.

"That time, I thought everything has gone to hell and there's no way I can ever bounce back again. But that's how we are made. Bouncing back from hell is our specialty, isn't it? What I am trying to say is, look at Cash now. Is he the same?"

I shake my head. He's confident, cocky and he's, well, *Cash*.

"Exactly. Am I the same girl I was when we used to play in your garage?"

"You're not daddy's princess anymore."

"Exactly. I had the best parents, a sheltered life. I don't know what putting effort into something or working hard was. Cash was a guy who lived the worst life with his parents, he had to work his ass off for everything he ever wanted or even needed. That's who we were but look at us now. Don't you think we have become the best version of ourselves?"

"Yeah, you have." I don't know where she is going with this but I like the story. It makes you feel happy and proud how much they have grown.

"That's because Cash and I love each other. We had our relapses but at the end of the day we wanted to become the best of what we can be for each other because they deserve it and we owe it to ourselves. I'm not forcing you to date Callen. It's not your obligation." Ver reaches out for my hand and holds it in hers. "But Ari, I have seen the way he looks at you. He wants to remove all the pain, fight your demons and give you a happy life. He's determined to make you his. He wants to work hard to get you even though you both are polar opposites."

Sincerity shines in her eyes. "And at the end of the day, someone who is ready to do that for you is who you need. You would be shocked at how beautifully love heals you. It really does. All you need is that one person who doesn't let your hand go as you become a whole and I think Callen is the one for you." She smiles softly.

Chapter 27

CALLEN

The loud music thumps in my ear as we take a shot. Edwin audibly cringes at the taste.

"Explain to me again why we are doing shots?"

"To loosen up, Eddie." Andrew slaps his back. "Look around us, this is our night."

"And the Celestials too." Cade pipes.

"Them too. But this is our first night as an up and coming band."

"First of many." I raise my shot and they all do too.

"First of many!"

Second shot in my system.

Today was the day we would mark in our calendars. Our song with The Celestials will be released tonight.

They have thrown the biggest and expensive release party I have ever seen.

"Hey boys." Lexa greets us happily. She has a sequin blue party dress on which made Andrew's mouth drop open.

Our 'hi's and 'hello's overlap.

"You all look dashing."

"Well, I wish I could say the same thing about you. You look phenomenal." Andrew drawls, looking her up and down and back up again.

Cade elbows him and he stifles a 'oof'.

"Why don't you come to meet the rest? I can introduce you to other singers." Her pink cheek huffs out as if she's trying to cool herself down.

"Sure." We detach from the bar and into the partying crowd.

Grinding bodies filled the dance floor and I recognized many famous singers, actors and influencers.

We trail behind Lexa and she takes us to a couple sitting together, whispering something to each other.

"Hey lovebirds." Lexa pats their backs and they turn. It was Ver and her boyfriend. *The Cash Flow.*

Edwin's mouth drops open. I am surprised he didn't faint at the sight of his favorite rapper.

"Hey guys." She smiles at us. She looks at me with a knowing gleam in her eyes. The same one she had when I was over at their house, cooking dinner for Aria. I interpret it as *I know something is going between you both but I will not ask about it* with a diabolical *hehe.*

"Oh you must be The Corruption," Cash gives a flashy grin.

"Yes, sir. It's really great to meet you." Cade giddily extends his hand and Cash shakes it warmly.

Cash always had a hint of pureness in his face. He seemed like a guy who believed in good and gave charity of million dollars for helping people out. He might use some very creative words in his songs but he always strikes me as a guy who has been through a lot and did quite a journey before reaching to the point he is in right now.

"We're huge fans." Cade says.

"And I'm your huge fan. I loved '*When You Believe*' and Vercy made me hear your new song with them. Just amazing." He makes an explosion gesture by his temple.

"It means so much to us. Thank you, Cash." I say genuinely. We have admired him for years and to even know that he listened to our songs is a huge compliment and accomplishment for us.

"Hey, aren't you Callen?" He points at me.

"Um, yeah?"

"Oh, you're *the* Callen." He says, laughing to himself.

Ver and Lexa both turn in shock to him.

"Babe, shut up." Ver swats his chest, horrified.

"Yeah, *babe*. Shut up!" Lexa adds with more intensity.

What is going on?

Ver turns to me, all smiles. "He just liked your vocals in the new song." She barks out a nervous laugh and my confusion.

"Oo...kay?"

"Oh, look." Lexa points at the huge clock in the bar. "It's almost 12. We better hurry."

"Right. Bye, babe." Ver kisses Cash on the cheek and rushes us to a stage they have installed.

"Where are we going?"

"To pop the champagne." Lexa shimmies onto the stage, taking the mic in her hand.

As Lexa entertains the crowd, I stand on the other side of the stage with Edwin. Andrew and Cade are on the opposite side with Ver and Zeenat.

The crowd erupts with laughter at the joke made by Lexa.

A finger pokes my side and I turn, startled to see who it was. A bright and smiley Aria looks up at me. She looks so genuinely happy that I can't help but smile myself.

"Hey stranger. Where have you been?"

"When you invite people, it's kind of your responsibility to entertain them. Sorry, I couldn't spend time with you or the boys."

164

"Hey, everything is good. Lexa and Ver accompanied us and we got to meet Cash Flow. *The* Cash Flow. Best day ever."

"You're releasing your second song today and meeting that idiot makes your day the best one?" Aria jokes.

"Cash is not an idiot!" Edwin gasps from my side.

"Idiot is said out of love, not intellectual sense." Aria covers up.

"Then okay." He goes back to watching Lexa.

"You look happy." I acknowledge. She couldn't stand still. It was like she was electrified with energy.

"Because this is the first song from our new album." She squeals. "And I'm releasing with my best friend. How can I not be happy, Cal?"

Cal. Cue butterflies.

I tuck a stray strand behind her ear and she stills.

"Did I tell you that you look beautiful today?"

"I think you forgot to mention that." She whispers, her eyes don't carry barriers this time, they're inviting.

My fingers trail her cheek. Her pink blush glows underneath my fingertips.

I want you, Aria.

"Without further ado, I call my friends on the stage, the Celestials and the Corruption."

My hand drops at the name. Aria bits her lips as she walks past us to the stage. We climb the stairs and the guests applaud, whistle and roar.

Aria takes the mic from Lexa.

"We would like to thank every single one of you for being here with us today. Your support means the world to us." A waiter hands her a champagne bottle, trading it for the mic.

We all huddled up with the bottle in hand, ready to pop it as the hands on the clock near 12am.

I was beside Aria. Luckily and fortunately.

"Thank you." I whisper to her.

"You need to be more specific." She says slyly.

"For taking a chance on my band, believing we were worth something."

Seven months ago, we watched their concert for the first time. Now, we are popping champagne with them for a new collab together. Life is really unpredictable.

"Believing is the best human trait."

"5, 4, 3..." The crowd countdowns.

"To many beautiful beginnings." I wasn't talking about the band. Not now. This is me and her. My endgame.

She pursed her lips before popping them out. She understands what I mean by the look in my eyes.

The wind blows, the breeze fluttering through her hair.

"To many beautiful beginnings." She agrees with a small smile and we pop the cork off.

Chapter 28

ARIA

"Ladies and gentlemen, we present you. The Celestials and The Corruption." Graham Silva introduces.
Applause greets our positioned body.

> *Light a fire in my eyes*
> *Take me on a ride*
> *Show me what is it like*
> *To be yours*
> *Do you promise you will be mine too?*
>
> *Two worlds collide when I'm with you*
> *Baby, hold my hand*
> *The night might have gotten away from us*
> *But we still have time*
> *Let me feel how it feels to be yours*
> *Light a fire into my heart and let me burn for you*
>
> *Look what have you done*
> *I can't sleep, I can't think*

You are everywhere
Running in my blood

I will cease to exist
With you

The song ends. We bow down and I couldn't fight the grin off my face. I almost forgot how amazing it was to perform.

The claps and the happy faces of the audience fills me with joy.

"Everyone, give it up for the amazing song done by The Celestials and The Corruption." Graham claps and another round of applause thunders. He leaves his seat to meet us.

"Lovely performance, girls." He kisses our cheeks. After coming to his show 3 times, we have gotten close.

"Thanks, Hams."

He goes on to meet The Corruption.

"Big fans, boys. Big fan." He shakes all their hands.

We descend the stage and walk to the main part of the talk show, the sitting area.

As we settle down, I feel Callen's body beside mine. There were long, U shaped couches. I was sitting after Zeenat, Lexa and Ver. Callen not so surprisingly chose to sit beside me. I didn't want to blush all through the interview.

I sneer at Callen and he grins at me.

"Bastard." I mouth.

"Beautiful." He spells out on his lips.

I turn, flushed towards Graham as he talks.

"The girls from Celestials have just released their first song from their album, *We exist* which collaborated with a brilliant upcoming band, Corruption, who are with us today."

Applause echoes.

"Tell us, girls, how did it feel to release your first song off the album?"

We had a code in our group. We pitch in when we want to. It's not like we have specific questions assigned to us. Talk shows are a way to show our personalities other than singing or concerts.

One eye contact with the girls and I know I'm answering this question.

"It was quite exciting actually. We met the Corruption all of a sudden and we instantly clicked with them. We became instant friends. Just like that." I snap my finger to emphasize the quickness.

"We even wrote our album with them."

"Little writing buddies." Edwin gestures like ahoy matey.

"I have been a fan of Corruption too. You released your first song 4 months ago and now you have a song with The Celestials, the most famous and adored girl band in this world. How does that feel?"

"Exhilarating, scary. Mostly amazing." Callen nods like he's saying facts. "They are the kindest, sweetest friends anyone can ask for." He turns to me, looking directing into my eyes. "They're angels."

Oh.

Graham notices Callen's little focus on me.

"Well, ever since the music video was released, Celestials beings and the Corrupt have taken many social media platforms to express something that they loved most in the video."

"Which is?" Andrew was too curious.

I already know what he is going to say. I saw the tweets.

"Callen and Aria." He bestows. "Your chemistry in the video is off the charts. You both just set the stage on fire with your duet." He gestures to the place we just performed. "So I will ask this question for every Celestial

169

being and Corrupted out there and myself. Are Aria Ryanne and Callen Cox dating?"

I let out a nervous laugh. "No, Graham. We aren't. We are close in terms of our love of music and common interest. He's my friend and I'm his friend."

Callen's eyebrows draw together at my answer. Graham goes on asking questions and I can't shake the feeling like I said something that Callen didn't agree with.

My heels are killing me. Is it even physically possible?

I was hobbling to my dressing room to change out. I left the girls back to talk to Graham. I really wanted to change out of this tight dress.

Even though I missed performing, our outfits were going to need some time to get used to.

Just as I near my dressing room, I hear giggles in the empty hallway. I frown as I reach the intersection. My eyes widen at who I see.

Callen and a girl.

She's twirling her hair and touching his arm. Callen was laughing at something she was saying.

Jealousy blooms in my chest at their close proximity.

Why the fuck are they standing so close to each other?

I clear my throat dramatically and the girl jumps at the sound and whips around.

Amusement dances in Callen's eyes as he sees me.

The girl is wearing a black T-shirt with *CREW* written on the back.

The nerve.

"I'm sorry. Am I *interrupting* something?"

"No, no. Summer was just telling me about herself. You want to join?" Callen grins.

"Oh really? Continue, Summer. I don't want to *interrupt* anything." I fold my hands, cocking a eyebrow at her.

Summer's face turns to the reddest shade of colour I have ever seen.

"You're not interrupting. I was just on my way." And she scurries off.

"Why you gotta be rude, Aria?" Callen tsks as he starts walking towards where I was standing.

"I'm sorry if I ruined your chances to get laid tonight." I scrunch my nose at him.

"You really think I wanted to sleep with her?"

I shrug obviously and turn around to march away. "You seriously don't know me then." He says from behind and my steps flatter for a second.

Would he have slept with her if I didn't interrupt? Or at least made out?

"Just admit Aria, you like me more than you let yourself to." He comes in the room with me.

I scoff. "That is so not true."

"Then why did you get jealous?"

I open my mouth to object but no voice comes for defending.

This only deepens his grin. He's enjoying this. The bastard he was.

"Go to hell, Callen."

"Would I find you there?"

"Oh, I thought I was your angel?"

"Angels are made in hell too." He says, entrapping me towards my dressing table. His hands on both sides of my waist.

My body heats up at how close he is to me. I lift my head, defiantly. Two can play this game. "Where do you think I am from?"

"Definitely hell. Because you know exactly how to make me suffer."

171

"Aw, someone is getting tired of chasing the girl he is infatuated with." I pout, inching closer to him.

Callen exhales forcefully like he can't get enough air out his lungs. With one swift move, he pushes me off my feet off the ground and unto the table, coming in between my legs. His fingers grip my thighs protectively.

"I would go hell and back for you. No question. And what I feel for you isn't infatuation, darling. It's more than that."

My next breath is audibly taken.

"See you soon, Angel." He presses his lips to my forehead.

The flutters and melodies start playing.

Chapter 29

ARIA

Today was our first show on our tour. Corruption was going to be our opening act but we ran into a problem. Problem being that they are a fucking mess.

Edwin is hyperventilating in a paper bag. Andrew is sweating, a lot. Cade is curled in Olivia's lap. The only thing he is not doing is sucking his thumb. And Callen, he's locked in the bathroom god knows doing what.

"Guys, c'mon. Cheer up. You're performing." I clap.

"I don't think I can." Andrew wipes his face with a tissue. "Did you even see the amount of people out in the arena? It's like the whole population of tiny China is there."

Biggest mistake: Letting them get coffee before the show. I told them that we had people to get what we want but they wanted fresh air so they went out anyways.

Look where it got them.

"Boys, get a grip of yourself." I plead again but it falls to no ears. They're anxious for their own good.

Olivia throws me an apologetic look and I sigh.

Only one person can help me. Only if he wasn't a mess like the others.

I knock on the washroom door.

"It's open," His voice comes from the other side. I twist the doorknob to see Callen sitting on the edge of the bathtub.

He sees me and greets me with a halfhearted smile.

"Big night." He says.

"It could be. If your band mates stop freaking out."

"I can't help them if I am feeling the same thing."

I sat in the bathtub beside him. "What is the matter, Callen? I thought you were looking forward to this."

"I was." He exclaims. "But when we went out there, we saw so many people. We're going to perform in front of the biggest crowd we've ever had. The most people we ever performed for was when Jackson kept chicken wings and beers night at the bar."

"Hey, what about when we performed at Graham's show?"

"There were like 30-40 people on that. Here we will have 30-40 thousand people. I'm scared if we mess up and disappoint you and the girls in one way."

"Oh, Callen." I put my hand around his shoulder. "You can never embarrass me or them. You know we trust you."

"But what if…"

"No 'what if', Callen. We know. When girls know something, they are hard on facts."

He laughs a sad laugh. "What if I'm not enough?" He says putting his head in his hands.

The air is heavy with somber. Callen was insecure of the talents he is good at. How does he even doubt himself?

I throw a leg over the ledge of the bathtub and sit inside.

Callen turns to follow my movement. "What are you doing?"

I pull my legs to my chest, tapping the remaining space left behind me. "Get in."

He looks at me in confusion but doesn't question as he gets in.

I loved his trust on me. He never questioned me in any way.

I bite my lip from smiling. He's way too big for the tiny tub.

"What is this about?"

"This is what helps me calm down. Whenever I'm anxious."

He arched his eyebrows. "Sitting in the bathtub."

"Everyone has their coping mechanisms." I try to reach to close the shower curtain in the teeny space.

"Here, let me help you." He reaches out and grabs my waist, pulling me to him.

"What are you doing?"

"Making sure there's enough room for both of us." I am sitting in between his legs, my back flushed against his chest.

"Is it necessary?"

"Absolutely."

I shake my head, proceeding to close the curtains. "You just need excuses to be near me, don't you?"

"There wouldn't be enough excuses for the level of closeness I want from you." He pulls me back so I am lying on his chest.

I didn't want to say anything because I liked this. The warm fuzzy feeling it gave in my chest. His strong hand wrapped around me. The body heat in these enclosed spaces.

"It makes me feel safe." I say after a while.

"What does?"

You. "This closed space. Whenever I feel scared or my nerves are out of control. I sit in the bathtub and close the curtains."

"Why, love?" His fingers caress my arms.

175

"I'm secluded from the rest of the world. When I am in the tub, no worry can harm me. I'm safe." I don't tell him how many times I wake up from a nightmare and the bathtub is the first thing I seek. It has become a safe haven for me.

"Are you scared now?" He asks, his thumb making a lazy circle on my wrist.

"Surprisingly, no."

"Because I'm here?" I can feel his grin behind me.

"You could be a fraction of the reason." I admit.

"Calm me down, will you? I have to perform in front of 40 thousand people in half an hour."

I chuckle, bringing his hand around me; I place it on my chest. He instantly stills. A very good reason for that might be his hand right between my boobs, but he asked me to calm him down.

"Can you feel it?" My heartbeat.

He hums into my skin.

"Close your eyes and count it."

We stay in silence as he counts my heartbeats. His leg doesn't have the tremor anymore and he's breathing evenly.

"Your heart," Callen says after a long time or does it feel that way? "It's beating so fast."

I wince in embarrassment. "Yeah, I was hoping you wouldn't notice that."

"Why not?"

I don't want to answer him.

"Is it because of me?" His lips were close to me. Very close.

Don't give too much credit to yourself, that's what I was going to say but all words leave my mouth as I turn my face to him.

We were inches away. If I crane my head a little forward, I can meet him in a place that I can't stop thinking about for months.

"You are amazing, Callen. You're smart, handsome and everything good in this world. Erase the doubt from your mind. You're going to do great." I whisper.

"Thank you for letting me in your favorite spot."

Little did he know that he had discovered the entrance to my castle, broken in, and patched it up so that no one else could ever enter. My heart ached with a strong feeling.

I think I like him more than I admit.

I close the distance between us. My lips to his. My soul to his.

Chapter 30

CALLEN

When I was in 5th grade, Mom made waffles for the first time in our house. When I ate it, I thought nothing could be better than eating waffles.

But I was wrong. Little did 9 year old Callen know that he would meet a girl 13 years later who would make him fly in a sky full of waffles. Who would rip his heart off his chest and claim it and I would bleed a happy man knowing that she owns my love.

Aria was the high. Aria is the hope in the morning sky. Aria is the necessity of my existence. She's mine and I'm hopelessly hers.

She kisses me like she wants to drink me up completely. *Same, baby, same.*

I twist her onto her front so we can kiss better. She's on her knees, bending to kiss me.

She feels like the altitude of the highest sky.

My hands trail from her hips to her bare legs. Her shorts were giving me easy access to the parts of her I wanted to devour. I squeeze her ass.

A moan escapes against my lips.

And damn if I wasn't getting turned on, second by second.

We are kissing again, our tongue are dancing on a languid style. Aria's hand trails down and under my shirt. I feel her hand on my skin and explicit images fill my head.

I growl, pushing my fingers into her hair.

"After the concert today, I am taking you to my room and I'm kissing you all night."

"Just kissing?" She arches her eyebrows at me teasingly.

"Baby, if you want me to do more than kissing, you have it." I kiss her, pulling her bottom lip between my teeth. "I will give you everything in the world, Angel. Just ask me for it."

She smiles and my heart soars. "Come on, we have a concert to do." She stands up, offering me her hand. Cute to think that she can actually pull me up. I hold onto her hand, getting up because I would grab on every opportunity to touch her.

"You're cute."

"I know." She answers.

She pushes off the curtains, letting the real world in.

Nothing seemed to change though. I wasn't letting her go in our bathtub haven or in the real world.

"Hey, Ari."

"Yeah?" She turns.

I pull her to me, giving her hopefully not the last kiss of this night. "I like you." I say against her lips.

179

ARIA

The crowd moves against the music. They are screaming, swaying, crying and doing what not.

I told my crew to finish my makeup first because I wanted to see the boys performing the opening act.

I lean against the cold metal pillar of the stage, looking at them. They were naturals. Sure, they were lazy sometimes and I had to scold them to do things but they were passionate about singing and they did it beautifully.

Callen was a huge help to get them on the stage. He lifted my words up when I was giving them a motivational speech. He agreed, he added, he helped.

He knew the boys better than I did so he nudged them dozen the right direction.

Callen hops off the platform, strumming his guitar.

Callen. I smile. *My* Callen.

I am never letting him go. Ever.

I still don't know what exactly I feel for him because I haven't felt this before. *Ever.* He is so damn special that the feeling comes with a warning to never let him go.

As if he could hear me thinking about him, he turns to me.

I'm sucked into his beautiful glistening face. A slow grin lazes on his lips as he continues to play his guitar.

I blow him a kiss and he grabs it out of the air. Laughter bubbles in my throat at his dorky gesture.

Andrew finishes his solo and Cade's drum builds up to the bridge.

Callen grabs on to his mic, his eyes on me.

Yeah, you know
Standing there like you're not the culprit
Like you didn't steal my heart
You kiss me and say we're just friends

180

Then girl, why don't you look into my eyes
and tell me you don't feel the butterflies
Because I am feeling them too
And I'm going to burst out of love one day
And soar the skies with you

You're lying to yourself
You know that you feel more than you pretend
You know, you know, you know

That you're falling, angel
And I'm right beside you
Falling with you

Chapter 31

CALLEN

"Good night." I wave to Cade, Olivia on my right and Andrew to my left.

"Are you sure you don't want to come to the after party?"

"Yes, I am." I say without thinking for a second.

"Are you okay, Callen?" Olivia asks, concerned.

"Yeah, I'm good. It's just been a long day. I'm tired."

"Rest well, buddy." Cade pats my shoulder and they leave.

Finally!

I close the door behind me.

When is she going to come? What if she doesn't come?

A knock resounds in the empty room and I nearly throw myself at it.

Talk about desperation.

I open the door calmly and I see her on the other side. Fuck keeping my cool, I want her right now.

"Hey." Aria steps in and I pull her to me. Closing the door behind her. I push her against the door, attacking her succulent lips. She fits her hands into my shirt, pulling me closer than we already are.

I enjoyed every single minute on her lips. The feel of her body on mine.

"Callen." She nibbles my lip. "Fuck me."

I growl, hoisting her up, legs wrapping around my waist as I carry her to the bed.

I gently lower us down and she starts grinding on my hard on. Every second was a torture with her.

She tugs on all my strings, making me fall harder for her.

I reach under her dress to remove her underwear only to feel her bare skin.

She breaks our kiss long enough for me to say, "You don't have underwear on."

"Why should I wear it when you're going to take it off me anyways?"

"You beautiful tease." I yanked her dress up.

She was sinful. I bend down to get a better view of her.

"You're so beautiful, Aria." I rub her thighs as I say. She's captivating. Her deep brown eyes take me in, soaking every inch.

Scraping my teeth with her belly button, she squirms beneath me. "Can I fuck you, Aria?"

She shudders at the question.

"Why is that a question, Cal?"

I spread her open with my fingers. My body is inflamed with how soaked my fingers become with one swipe.

"You wanna know something?" I ask, kissing her inner thigh.

She hums in response.

"I love it when you call me Cal."

And I dive in.

"Oh, Callen." A moan falls out of her pretty mouth when my tongue takes the first swipe. She coats my tongue.

I flatten my tongue on her clit, switching between long languid strokes and fast ones that made her toe curl.

"You taste so good, Aria. You taste like you're made for me." With that, I insert a finger into her.

Her hips buck up and I know it's too much for her but I want her to come and I want to make her come till she is seeing stars.

"Callen." She is gripping the sheets, knuckles white.

"Yes, sweetheart?"

"I'm going to come." She whimpers, pushing her fingers into my hair.

"Come for me, baby."

And does come for me. Screaming with pleasure and tugging on my hair. Her legs are thrown over my shoulders as I feasted on her, chasing her down her high.

I come up as she tries to catch her breath. Her cheeks are flushed, heaving.

"Hey."

She smiles. "Hi."

I kiss her and she peeks her tongue to taste me, indirectly tasting her. My cock throbs in my pants.

"Tell me, Ari. What position would you liked to be fucked in first?"

"From behind." She says, pulling my lower lip between her teeth.

"Your wish is my command, Angel." I just get off her for split second to take the condom from my night drawer.

Aria sits on her elbows, watching me. "You were planning for this?"

"Anticipating this." I corrected her. "But just so you know, I have had a condom packet in my wallet since we met so I was more like dreaming."

She laughs. I remove my pants and boxers, rolling on a condom. Aria is following my every move with her hungry eyes.

"On your knees and elbows, baby."

She shifts her position as I come behind her.

"Grab the headboard, Aria. You might need something to hold on to."

She listens to me, clutching the headboard with her long fingers.

I position my cock right on her entrance and with one swift move, I'm in.

We both groan at the same time. My eyes almost rolled into my head at the pleasure that courses in me.

I thrust deeper in her as we get accustomed to each other. I can feel how deep I am into her pussy with my hand on her abdomen.

Taking her this way was an entryway to heaven and I wanted to fuck us both into oblivion.

Aria stretches herself like a cat, jutting her ass higher and deeper into my cock. We make eye contact in the mirror in the headboard and I see the naughty gleam in her eyes as she starts rolling her ass on my pelvis.

My fingers involuntarily dig into her hips so hard that I think I bruised it.

But she deserves it for being such a tease.

"Give me your hands, Aria."

Molten heat flows her eyes as she pushes her hand back, locking it behind her. Something about the heat in her eyes, the dripping of her pretty pinky pussy and me being so deep in her, awakened an animal in me.

I grab her hand, pulling her body up with it. She flushes against my chest. With her locked in my grasp, I start thrusting in and out.

Her head lulls to the side and I take the opportunity to mark her neck.

"Do you know how hard you make me? How just the sight of your round ass getting pounded by my cock is enough for me to come?" I whisper into her ears, swiping two fingers down her pretty face. She takes them into her mouth, sucking them.

I groan silently at the feeling. She might have seen my reaction to her in the mirror because I feel her smirk. "What are you thinking, Callen?"

I don't want to answer her because she knows what I am thinking. *Her pink lips on my cock.*

"You want me to suck you, baby?" She teases. "We can do it after round 2."

She talks dirty. She fucks dirty. And I am so close to coming.

I flip her over. Her hair is thrown into beautiful curls. I come between her legs and she welcomes me by wrapping her legs around me.

I think about the last time when I was between her legs. In the dressing room at Graham's show. She denied her feelings for me but also got jealous when I was talking to the stage girl.

My Aria is possessive and there's no one I would rather be with than her.

"You know what I think you are?"

"What?"

"You're selfish."

She laughs, arching her back. "What gave that away?"

"You want to keep me all to yourself. You won't bear as much as the sight of someone close to me, can you?"

We switch positions. Aria is the one who initiates it.

She positions herself above my cock, letting me enter her again. She moves hard on me.

Her fingers dig into my shoulder and abdomen as she rides me.

"Yes, I am selfish. Yes, I want you all to myself. Because I can't stand the idea of you kissing and fucking someone who isn't me."

I sit up, positioning her even better so she gets me deeper. "Why?"

I see hesitation in her face. "Tell me why."

She's opening up to me and even though its sex, I know she's saying the truth.

"Because." She can barely get the word out of her mouth as we both yearn for the release, pleasure clouding our minds.

"Because?"

"Because I can give anyone the world but I can't bear it if they take away my world from me." She says as orgasms.

She clenches around me, making me come too.

I relax back into the bed, taking Aria with me. We are silent for two minutes. My mind is still trying to cope up with what she said.

I'm her whole world?

I almost hear her thoughts when she whispers against my chest. "I am not selfish but when it comes to you, I can't help it."

Chapter 32

ARIA

I feel his fingers skim the length of my arms before reaching my hand and intertwining our fingers together.

A kiss on the shoulder turns into millions of them on me.

I laugh, finally opening my eyes to the light. The sun was rising and my heart was full of an emotion I didn't recognize but loved feeling this way.

"Good morning." Callen's raspy voice whispers into my neck before leaving a kiss there too.

I turn my body towards him with a lot of struggle. My body ached from what we did last night and that I was jumbled with Callen's large hand, his leg pinning mine and comforter cocooning us.

I come face to face with Callen smiling at my struggle to turn and a smile breaks out on my lips too.

"Good morning."

"Indeed it is. Every morning is a good morning if I wake up next to your beautiful face and your warm naked body."

I bite my lip. "We should really talk about last night."

"Okay."

"Does this change anything between us?"

"In our relationship as partners, a little bit. Every time you would be in the studio, I might want to take you on the couch itself."

"How modest of you."

"Who am I kidding? I can never get enough of you."

"Callen, I don't want this to end." I say all of the sudden. His hand freezes in the back before he pulls me closer to him. "Did I scare you off?"

"Never, Angel. I was just surprised by your honesty. You know that you're not much of an open person."

"I will work on that."

"You don't need to. I love figuring you out. It shows me sides of you I wouldn't have imagined."

"Is it a good thing?"

"Very good thing." He tucks my hair behind my ear. "Aria, I like you a lot. More than that maybe but let's not climb that ladder now. What I do know for sure is that you feel right. So right. When I kissed you, when we had sex, I loved every second of it because you were in it. I have no idea what the future holds for us but let me assure you what we have is something that cannot be ended. Angels don't leave their broken people."

I massage my thumb over your hand. "But you're leaving today."

This was the only opening act they would do for our tour. Today, they would leave for Nashville for a concert of their own and Celestials would continue their tour. None of the cities which we are touring matches theirs. We are going two separate ways.

"Two months aren't a huge deal. I mean, it's a humongous deal for me because I can't be with you but I will console my poor heart."

I laugh a little. "You sure?"

"Very sure. I believe in us, Aria. Even if there's a little chance that we could be together, I will work on it, putting my heart and soul into it." He tugs me closer as if our close proximity does not satisfy.

"How do you believe so much? Isn't it exhausting?"

"Because believing is the best human trait. We should believe more often. That's what makes us humans and that's how humanity exists."

"Okay, chill out there. I didn't sleep with you for your philosophical ass."

"I know. You slept with me for my humor and skills in bed-" I put a hand over his mouth with a horrified expression on my face.

"Shut up."

His eyes crinkle and body vibrates with laughter.

I shake my head, removing my hand from his mouth.

He takes it back and kisses it. "I'm going to miss you."

I kiss his chest, laying my head on it. His heart is starting to pick up its pace. "I already miss you."

Chapter 33

ARIA

The humid air welcomes me as I step out of the airport terminal. My glasses fog up in an instant. It slipped out of my mind that I was wearing them myself.

I remove them, still searching in the crowd. We got taken from the exit of the airport so we didn't need to encounter the raging crowd gathered in the front, waiting for us.

"Ma'am, this way." The huge dude says, walking with us. If I had a dollar for every time we had a different face every time to protect us when we came back.

Hope stirred in my chest. I really didn't expect him to come, did I? Maybe he is in the house, waiting for me. Or maybe he will bring the boys later to meet us.

I was allowed to hope. We spent the best 2 months together and we didn't even meet each other during that time. It was just text messages, FaceTime and flowers at my hotel room.

Eventually I had to tell the girls that he and I finally made a move. The flowers were filling up my room. They were way too happy for their own good. I felt like I was bringing their hopes up for something that will crash and burn eventually but a part of me–a huge part- wanted to keep pretending. Acting like this is what I wanted even though from inside I was terrified of us. We might become something good that would soar the skies or something that will wreck us permanently.

I was playing a dangerous game here.

"Oh my god, he didn't!" I hear Lexa squeal in front of me.

I don't understand her source of excitement till I see it myself. Two black cars in the parking lot. Callen leaning against the SUV.

The air in my lungs dissipates at the sight of him. Callen was relaxed back, hair shining under the sun with an easy smile on his face, looking at us. His eyes find me and he is detaches himself from the car.

A strangled crossover between a cry and a laugh bubbles in my throat. I drop the suitcase in my hand and rush forward.

Callen meets me halfway.

Tears sprung out of my eyes.

"I missed you." I say, muffled in his neck. I fucking missed him so much. I forgot how used to him I became when we were not spending every second of the day together.

"No more missing, angel. I'm here." He kisses my forehead.

"No tour for a year." I mumble, promising as he wipes away the tears from my cheek.

"Your fans wouldn't like it but it's more than fine with me." He smiles, cupping my face and just like that my day gets brighter and better.

What is happening to me?

Chapter 34

CALLEN

Never in my life have I yearned for someone's touch so much. She buries her head and I can feel her tears on my neck which bring tears in my own eyes.

I missed her. I missed her so goddamn much. And I promise right there and then, standing in the airport that there is no way I am ever letting her away from me ever again. I rather follow the whole world with her than stay a minute apart from her.

Edwin and Andrew finish meeting the girls. As they load their luggage in their car, they take Aria's too.

"No, wait. That will go in my car."

Edwin looks at me in confusion. "But it's the same destination right?"

"Just put it in my car, man."

Andrew whispers something into Edwin's ear and a cheeky smile comes on his face.

"The luggage goes in your car, highness." He gestures dramatically and puts her suitcase in my car.

Aria is talking to her band mates in the distance. I couldn't hear much but it looked like they were teasing her and she was burning red.

"I bet he has planned-" Ver starts. A howl of the wind carries away the remaining sentence.

"Please, shut up. He's right there. He might be handsome but he isn't deaf."

"After having you in his bed, he will become deaf soon."

'Oh Callen' A teasing moan erupts through their group and my body shakes with laughter.

Aria stomps away, coming to me. Her face is blushing with embarrassment.

"I don't like them." She huffs as they continue laughing in the distance.

"You love them. Even if they make some quite right observations."

Aria's mouth falls open. "I'm not *that* loud." She swats my chest.

I catch her wrist, pulling her to me. "You are loud when my cock is destroying you."

Heat flares her dark brown irises. "But they are all mine, angel. I want to consume all your little gasps, all your moans. You are mine to be listened to and taken by."

"We are loaded!" Andrew announces shutting the door.

"You will be riding with me." I release her wrist as I open the door for her. Aria's hand shivers in anticipation as she nods. She bids goodbye to the girls and sits in the car.

I go to my side as she is plugging in her seatbelt.

"What's the plan for today?" Aria asks, relaxing back into her seat. I cooled the car for her before itself. It was way too hot outside and humidity could almost choke you.

I wrap my fingers around her chin, pulling her perfect face to mine. "I will take you to my apartment."

"Then?" She hits my nose with hers.

"Make you breakfast."

194

A small smile comes on her face. She likes the idea.

"Then?" Her voice had a seductive tone to it, and she was out of breath.

"We do whatever is in your mind now." With that, I kissed her after 2 months.

She starts kissing me as soon as I open the door. We push into the apartment. Her hips hit the dining table and she slides into it.

Aria's fingers start fumbling with my buttons. I caught her hand, stopping her. *What the hell is wrong with you, Callen?*

"Breakfast." I whisper into her lips. I try to move away but she wraps her legs around me. "We can have breakfast later after a while. Maybe after, I don't know, 20-30 minutes."

My eyes widened at the duration while Aria's dance with pure heat and mischief. She was suggesting rounds, many of them.

"Don't tempt me. You came back from a long trip and I know you didn't eat anything on the plane. Breakfast and then whatever you want. I promised you, didn't I?"

"Better keep your promise, Cox."

"Boy scouts honor, Bastian."

She jumps off the table, removing her jacket and shoes by the door.

I go to the kitchen to start preparing.

"Hey, where's your washroom?"

"Down the hall, first door to your right. That will be my bedroom. There's an attached washroom there." I call from the kitchen.

"Okay, thanks." I hear her footsteps receding.

I whip out egg and bacon from the fridge. Despite all the boasting I did about making breakfast, my cooking skills weren't the best. I did make decent food but most of it is basic.

I don't know if Aria will like it or not.

I neglect that thought. She will like it. She's a person who even though might not like it, she will still eat it to not upset me. I just hope she doesn't do that. I don't want my girlfriend to have bad food. The saying, something is better than nothing, really applies here?

I pour the egg into the pan as bacon sizzles in the other.

A pair of hands encircles my torso. A chin reaching to my shoulder.

"Can I help?"

"You can actually." I say, turning. I carry her up to the counter beside the stove.

"Sit your pretty ass here and tell me everything about the tour."

"I mean, if you insist." She shrugs laughing.

Aria starts telling about all the places they visited. Crazy and sweet fans they met. I ask her questions, sometimes to elaborate, sometimes to confirm.

I could listen to her for hours. Hand gestures, sweet laughs and jokes with impersonating voice were her thing and I loved it.

The food was done cooking and I suggest to sit in the balcony. I wanted Aria to see the view from there.

"So, I was thinking…" I start.

"What *were* you thinking?" She teases as she takes a bite of the bacon.

God, I had no idea how to ask her.

"Umm," I elongated.

She reaches out for my hand. "Hey, don't hesitate."

"I know we haven't put a tag on us yet and honestly, we don't even need to. As long as I'm with you, I'm happy. But then, this weekend, me and my family are having one of our monthly dinners and I was hoping if it's okay with you, I want you to come with me."

"You want me to meet your family?" Her tone is undetectable.

"Not for getting their blessing for married or anything. Well, not at least now. I mean, no labels till we decide on it. I just would like you to be there with me." I cover up, nervously.

"Callen, I would love to come but the thing is, I'm not very good with families."

"You had one of your own, right?" I meant to say it in a way to lighten the mood but her eyes turned sad and liquidly.

"And how did that end?" She squeaks, thick with emotions.

"Oh no. Aria, *no*. What happened to your family was a horrible tragedy. I promise my parents or siblings will not ask you about it. I know you miss your family like hell and I understand that. I couldn't even imagine how I would live my life without my family. You went through a horrible thing, baby and I can't undo the hurt, no matter how much I want to. But can I suggest something to you? Why don't you take my parents as your parents' figures in your life? What's mine is yours. I know it sounds a lot like the wedding vows but when I say it, I mean it. I'm not forcing you to come but if you do and if my family can make you feel even a fraction of happiness you deserve then I would call it a win." I blabber a lot but I hope what I said goes through her. I hold her hand in mine, squeezing it with assurance. "Just think about it."

"Just your parents and siblings will be there?"

"Absolutely. Dad, mom, Missy and Cam."

"I would like to meet the famous sarcastic Missy." Aria smiles.

Oh, thank god. I didn't realize I would kill to just see her smile until now.

"And hear Cam's weird sex stories." I remind her.

197

She laughs now. "Yeah, that too."

"So is that a yes?"

"It is." She scrunches her nose happily. "I hope I don't screw it up."

I reach over the table, pecking her lips. "I hope *I* don't screw it up. You're perfect."

"I highly doubt that, sweetie."

I sit back on my seat. "We can argue about that all day long but why don't we finish eating and get you some sleep?"

"That's not how I remember the list going."

Oh wait, yeah. How can that slip out of my mind? For the last 2 months, I missed the hell out of her and her alluring body. The temptation intensified every day because all we got was one night together. It wasn't enough. The hunger for her was intense.

"Next thing on the list it is." I wink at her.

Chapter 35

ARIA

I was brushing my teeth when the door opened and I heard footsteps in the room.

"Need any help?" Callen calls from the bedroom.

"For brushing? No, thank you."

I can feel his smile through the door.

I spit into the sink and rinse my mouth. After I was done washing and drying my face, I came out of the washroom.

Callen is on his phone, sprawled over the bed. I stand by the washroom door, admiring him. He changed into sweatpants. And was shirtless.

If my mouth didn't salivate at that point itself.

My Callen.

He hears my thoughts as he raises his head to look at me. He narrows his eyes playfully. "Why were you taking so long? I missed you."

I walk over to him and straddle him. "How very clingy." I tsk as I let my hands roam his upper body.

"I would be your koala." He breathes out.

"Koala?"

"Koalas cling on each other."

"They cuddle, sweetie."

"Wait, really?"

"Yes." I kiss his neck and travel down. "Don't worry, you're still my koala."

"See, that's why I am dating you. No girl would call me her koala when she is kissing me."

"I'm the only girl who gets to." I flick my tongue over his nipple and he groans.

"There's no one before you and no one after you. You have spoiled me for every other person out there." Callen trusts me as he takes my hand and keeps on his heart. "This beats for you only, my angel."

Emotions overcome me. I lean down to kiss the spot. "You already know who my heart beats for."

"Really, who?" He teases.

"Andrew Garfield." I reply cheekily and am immediately thrown on my back as he towers over me.

"You brat." He bites my chin.

"You bastard."

"What's your plan for today? Are you gonna tease me or you're gonna let me make love to you the whole day?"

"Hmm, let me think." I act as if I'm thinking but when he surges his hips into me and the feeling has me rolling my eyes back into my head.

"We can foreplay later." I say, bringing his mouth to mine.

As we fuse, we ignite.

Slowly, slowly, he strips me off while he wears a sorry excuse of sweatpants.

"Remove." I tug on the waistband of his sweatpants.

"Anything for you, love."

There are no barriers between us as we mold into each other.

"Listen." He says as he takes my nipple in his mouth.

I hum in response as I wiggle in pleasure underneath him.

"I like you."

"You do?"

"Can't feel otherwise."

I knew he was feeling something greater than that but he is trying to not scare me away.

"I really like you too."

"You do?"

"I do, Cal." I intertwine my fingers into his hand.

Whenever we had sex, that wasn't the only thing we did. We were vulnerable to each other. And moments with him are when I am not afraid to open my heart.

"You have no idea how happy that makes me." He grins as he kisses me for the hundredth time and I melt again.

"I have something in mind, actually."

"Hmm? Like what?"

"Wait." He slides off me and rummages in the drawer and I thought he was taking out condoms but he pulls out air pods.

I frown as he pulls his phone off the side table.

He fidgets something on the phone and I can't keep myself from asking him.

"What are you doing?"

"Just plug this in." Callen says as he inserts ear buds into my ears. I immediately hear Chase Atlantic.

"Concentrate on the music, angel." His mouth moves as he bends over to peck my collarbone. It goes below and below.

Teasing and sucking my nipples, swirling tongue over my belly button and finally to the place where I ached.

He slowly inserts a finger into me and my hips buckle.

I was so fucking tight.

"Haven't you been taking care of yourself?" Callen's voice asks me through the music.

"Stretch me out then." I try to speak as I grind my hips on his hand.

He inserts two fingers into me as he pumps in.

I was always so responsive to his fingers and mouth. I almost go out of my mind when he takes his fingers out of me.

I glower at the contact. But my body ignites again.

Callen spreads the wetness on my nipples, pinching them.

Without any protest, he knew what to give me.

He fucks me with his fingers and encloses his mouth on the wetness on my breast.

I moan and gasp at the sensation.

His mouth, his fingers, Chase Atlantic's song in my ears. I lose control in mere seconds as I come.

He slowed his pace but doesn't stop until I came down from my high.

I am a sweaty, gasping mess when Callen kisses me.

"I can't believe I get to be yours." He whispers on my lips. "I can't believe that I get to kiss you, I get to make you come, I get to listen to your sexy moans and taste you."

"I'm yours too." Tenderness coats me.

"This is so much better. You being mine and me being yours. You're my salvation, Aria Ryanne. You undone me. You ignite me. You are my angel. You are my forever."

Chapter 36

CALLEN

I turn off the car engine and turn towards Aria on the seat beside me. She's wearing a light blue dress, her hair which she recently cut, let down.

God, she's so beautiful.

"Hi." I nudged her with my elbow.

"Hey."

"You okay?"

"I'm nervous."

"Yeah, I figured." She taps her feet when she is nervous.

"Callen." She groan.

"Hey, look at me. They're gonna love you. Mom would lose her mind that I have a girlfriend. Dad is a huge fan of yours. Cam would try to hit on you but I will save you, don't worry and Missy considers you as her role model. Does this sound like a family that could remotely even think a negative thought about you?"

She is getting convinced by my words, I can see it on my face. I need to give a little push.

"Have you never met a guy's family before?"

"Never."

I stare at her in slight shock and she interprets it.

"I have never dated someone as long as I dated you."

"So you never reached this step in the relationship with any guy?"

She shakes her head. No wonder she is so nervous. *I'm her first proper boyfriend.* I grin at the thought.

"Don't gloat."

"I'm not gloating. I just feel special." I kiss her cheek.

"You *are* special, rock star."

"So are you, angel."

"I don't feel like vomiting from our cheesiness. Being with you is really rubbing on me."

I laugh.

"This might sound a bit cheesy but I think you are really *grate.*"

She rolls her eyes, opening the car door. "That was the last straw, I'm breaking up with you." She leaves the car and I follow her, laughing.

I am holding her hand as I knock on the door. "You're amazing."

She bites her lips, smiling.

"I like you." I kiss her cheek and that's when the door swings open. An ear splitting squeal basically splits my left eardrum.

"Oh my god, they're making babies on the porch."

A laugh bubbles out of Aria.

"I don't know whether your parents had the bees and the birds talk with you till now but that's not how babies are made." She extended her hand to Missy and my little sister had that much manners in her to shake her hand. Maybe I underestimate how civil she can be. "You must be Missy."

"You have no idea how much I am freaking out inside but all this is a cool exterior is a facade. I'm so excited to meet you. Big fan."

We step in the house and the delicious spices waft up my nose.

"Mom, Dad. The power couple are here." Missy announces and I hear shuffling in the kitchen before Mom pours out.

Her eyes go to Aria and she instantly melts into a puddle.

"Hi, darling." She goes straight for a hug. Mom is shorter than Aria so Aria had to bend to hug her.

"It's so nice to meet you, Mrs. Cox. You have a very beautiful home here."

"Thank you, honey." Mom tucks Aria's hair behind her ear as a sign of affection, swiping a hand over her head.

Aria closes her eyes, soaking it in.

Mom meets me next. "Cal, how are you?" She kisses my forehead. I had to bend 2 feet to let her do that.

"I'm good, Mom."

"You should be great. You brought such a special girl home."

Aria points to herself as she mouths teasingly, *"I'm special"*

I smile. She is becoming comfortable.

"Where's Dad and Cam?"

"In the dining hall. Setting the napkins and plates." Mom points her thumb to our dining hall.

"Let me introduce you to them." I help Aria with her coat and hang them in the rack with mine.

All this time, I haven't let go of her hand.

As we walk to the dining hall, I hear Mom say to Missy. "Look at them. That's what love is. They both look at each other like they're each other's worlds."

Aria's face shows that she heard what Mom said but for a girl who isn't in the rush to put labels on relationships, she seems okay with it. Blushing even.

She's warming up to the idea of us. She likes us.

"There are the lovebirds." Dad announces as he sees us entering.

"Hey Dad."

"Good evening, Mr. Cox."

"Good evening to you too, Aria. Please don't call me Mr. Cox. Dad is okay." He jokes.

Cam comes into the dining hall with silverware.

His mouth hangs open as he sees Aria.

"R & B?"

"Cameron?" Aria asks, equally shocked.

"Holy fuck, you're Aria from The Celestials."

"Language, Cam." Dad says deadpan as he takes the silverware from him.

"And you're Cam, Callen's brother."

"That I am."

What in the freaking hell? "You both know each other?" I ask.

"So almost a year ago, Zeenat met with an accident. Cameron is the one who did her surgery." She explains.

"Damn, Cam."

"I didn't know you guys were famous singers. How?"

"We had our own ways to conceal our identity."

"No wonder I wasn't allowed to treat her after a week. Your friend."

"We got our personal doctors, by then." Aria shrugs.

"Personal doctors? You guys are fancy."

I can't believe that Cam and Aria know each other. "Is that why you ran out of the meeting in a hurry?"

Aria frowns a little at my question. "How do you know about that?"

"Let's just say, I was there."

She raises her eyebrows, surprised.

"How's the girl?" Cam takes her attention before Aria could ask me anything.

"She's good. She has kept up with the doctor's appointment and everything is fine. I know I have said this in the hospital already but thank you so much for saving her." Vulnerability hints at her voice. Zeenat is very

206

special to her. She was her sister's best friend. They share the same loss.

"It's what I worked hard for." Cam pats her arm good natured. *Shocking.*

"Who wants goulash?" Mom comes into the dining hall, announcing grandly.

The warm breeze of the air sweeps over us. Aria is beside me laughing at something Missy said.

I pull her closer to me, nestling my nose to her hair and leaving a kiss there.

I liked this.

Her, me, the world.

They both look at each other like they are each other's world.

She is my world.

I swipe a finger over her elbow and her body shivers against mine. I smirk.

"Oh, it's 11:30." Aria notices. I still haven't moved away from here. I don't want to. "I'm sorry to stay this long. And I'm pretty sure you all have things to do tomorrow."

"No worries, dear. We loved having you over so much that we even lost track of time." Mom waves her concern off.

"Thank you so much for inviting me over. I better get going." Aria tries to move and then lets out a breezy laugh. "Callen?"

I open my eyes to her beautiful ones looking at me with amusement. "Yeah?"

"Drop me till the door?"

"Of course." I get up, her hand in mine.

"Did you enjoy today? I'm sorry if Mom was too imposing." I say as we get to the porch.

"Asking about our future babies and their names is not imposing at all." She teases.

I laugh, swiping a finger over her cheek.

"Thank you so much for bearing with them."

"Thank you so much for bringing me with you here. I needed this."

"Anytime." I pull her by the waist, kissing her.

Her lips are so familiar but I want to keep exploring them. She warms me in the cold evening air.

"I should really get going." Aria says between the kisses.

"Stay the night."

"I have a meeting tomorrow."

"I will drop you."

"No, it's fine. I will sleep in my bed but with you, there's not much sleep, is there?"

"I never heard you complain."

"It never was." She stands on her toes, pecking my lips. "I need sleep and I need to go to the meeting in the morning. Let me know when you get back home after the weekend."

"I will." I didn't want to let her go but I had to. "I'm going to miss you. Call me as soon as you reach home, okay?"

"How very clingy." She jokes and I swat her butt.

She giggles in my arms.

"Be careful. Keep the headlight on all the time. Drive slowly. Even if the road is empty, doesn't mean you increase the speed, okay?"

"Cal, baby. I will be fine. Not my first time driving at night."

"I still worry." I pout.

Aria wraps her hand around my neck and kisses the pout away. "It's cute that you worry about me and for you, I will be careful. Okay?"

"Thank you." I touch her collarbone with my lips and she inhales sharply.

"Bye before I ask you to take me on the porch of your childhood house."

I laugh as she runs away

"Callen?" She calls me from the car.

"Yes, angel?"

"I like you too."

Chapter 37

ARIA

The house stands alone on dried out grass. I haven't come to this house in 4 years but every day since that night, I carry the keys in my pocket, hoping that an opportunity presents itself where I was gladly forced to go in.

And today, I am going to open the door.

The rocking chair on which my mother sat when Astra and I used to play in our front yard was right on our porch.

A fleeting picture of a kind, loving mother reading her book. Her skin so soft, looking over at two daughters running and tackling each other in shrieks of laughter, imagining how they both would grow up to be the most beautiful girls and lead a life that would make them happier than they have ever been.

She was gone before she saw us living. The picture slips away and I learned to not chase after it.

I take that one key that stood out in the bunch of keys and insert into the keyhole, twisting it. The door creaks open. The air is thick with a musty, stale odor. It's dark inside with a hint of light coming from the neighbor's backyard and the remains of the moon.

Every fiber and cell in me is telling me to shut the door and never come back here again.

But I shouldn't.

Spending the evening with Callen's family made me miss mine. I rarely visited their graves, I haven't seen Dad from a long time and the last time I stepped into this house was the night of their accident. I left the very next day and stayed with Lexa till we moved in our house together.

Without a second doubt, I step in.

The crowd is alive. The energy is buzzing every atom in the air.

"Midnight memories, oh oh oh oh oh."

"Everybody." Lexa cheers and everybody claps, singing the lyrics with us.

A smile passes between me and Ver. Fridays are exceptionally full in Marco's bar and today's crowd is enjoying us.

"Thank you everyone." We had only a limit of 3 songs every night.

Applause vibrates through the space as we clear out the stage.

"Amazing performance, girls." Marco says as we sit at the bar stools.

"Thanks, Marc." He sets 4 cokes for us.

My phone buzzes in my jeans. I pulled it out. Mom.

I cast one glance on my friends.

Zeenat is talking to Marco. Lexa is flirting with a guy who looks like he is in college. Ver is smiling and typing on her phone. I bet on my dollars that it's Cashmere.

I go outside to pick up the call.

"Hey, Mama."

"Aria Rye, where are you?"

"In Marco's bar. Mama, you won't believe how amazing the crowd was today."

"Obviously they would be amazing, darling. You are singing for them." I smile at her words.

"Mama, I know I don't say this enough but thank you. Thank you for being so supportive for your 17 year old to play in a bar."

Mama laughs. "Even if you put like that also, I am still going to support you. You're my daughter and a born singer."

I swallow. My mom is my biggest believer and my biggest blessing. "Where's Astra?"

"She's out with her friends. She will pick me up on the way back."

"Still at the supermarket?"

"Yeah, you want me to get something for you?"

"Can you get me cookies?" I ask cheekily.

"Sure thing."

"I will be home soon, okay?"

"Okay, dear. Don't talk to strangers." She starts.

I completed it. "Don't pee in public washrooms and don't take a lift from someone you don't know. Got it." She always had a set of rules that I heard so many times that it has become a motor memory.

"Good girl. Be safe, I will meet you at home."

"Love you, Mama."

"I love you more, Aria Rye."

Lexa is drunk off her ass. Zeenat helps me carry her to my car.

"Good show, A." Zeenat says. She was Astra's friend. It might be a little weird to have your elder sister's friend in your band but we needed a backup singer and a drummer. Zeenat did both and did it good. So we took her in the band.

212

"Mom said that Astra has gone with her friends. Why didn't you go?"

"We had a gig." She states.

"I know genius. But afterwards, you could have gone, right? I don't want Astra to think that I am hogging her best friend." I close the backseat door on sprawled Lexa.

"We are going to brunch tomorrow. Don't worry."

"Send me breakfast through Astra's hands." I wave bye to Ver and Zeenat and start driving to Lexa's house.

Nobody is at her house. Her parents were most probably at some fancy ass event, scouting potential investors for their oil company.

I take the key from underneath the flower pot and unlock the door.

I carry Lexa to her bedroom. After making sure, she's all tucked in and her heels are off, I keep a glass of water and Advils I found in her mom's medicine cabinet. I lock the door on the way out and keep the key back in its place.

I'm back into the car. It's not until I turn the street from Lexa's house that my phone starts to ring.

The caller ID is titled as Unknown.

"Hello?"

"Aria." Voice says and the familiarity hits me.

"Dad?"

"Yes, dear."

"Why are you calling me this late at night?" Ever since he and Mama separated, we spoke and texted each other to update about our lives. We sometimes even met for cotton candy.

We maintained our father-daughter relationship. Not the one where you get to see your dad after he comes back home after a long day but one where your dad who picks you up to spend a day with him in his tiny apartment.

When the divorce papers filed were into the court, they took a part of what the way life was away with it.

"Aria." The word pained him to say it out. *I never heard him call me that way.* *"There has been an accident."*

214

Chapter 38

ARIA

There's been an accident.

Easy how one sentence can turn your life upside down.

I reached the hospital that they were taken to. I saw my Dad. We hugged after so long and cried for the two lives that fought to stay alive in the operating unit.

The doctor came out after a while and told us that they couldn't make it.

4 words. A declaration. They couldn't make it. That's it. He said he was sorry.

But was he though? Or was it a mechanical response to all bad things in the world?

I ran out. Out of the operation theater. Out on my dad and the bodies which once upon a time were my mom and sister.

My heart ached.

For myself. I was alone.

My dad. He didn't have his wife and first child anymore.

For everyone who went through the same shit I did.

I went home because that's all I had after the whole world was stolen from me. I sought refuge in my garage, my safe haven. I used to write songs. Mama used to sit in a black stool and listen to us when my band practiced. The pride in her eyes and the smile on her lips as she cheered us was an image that dug itself deeply in my mind.

She really believed I would make it. She told me that she was proud of me.

As I think back, I remember everything happening simultaneously. But it felt for the longest time. I suffered. It was too much for a 17 year old to take.

I take knowing steps inside of the house, to the garage. I don't go in but stand on the threshold and look.

It was barely there anymore. The walls are charred and black. Nothing left except lingering memories that hung in the air.

A void opened in my heart and it keeps expanding. I go to the only place that has none of this shit from the world. Maybe it won't be true. Maybe they are playing a prank on me.

They had to be alive, right? They can't just leave me alone. They love me...

Garage door opens and I step inside. This place carried life, music and love. It carried all my happy times, my songs, her laughter.

Where is it now? When I need it the most.

Mama watched my practice with my band. Astra bought us snacks and made fun of our breakup songs.

Where are they?

Something fills me. A shift.

The sorrow, the funniness in my chest turns into something red.

Fury. Anger.

This isn't fucking fair. Nothing is.

I march to the kitchen and bang open the drawers, finding what I am looking for.

I find it.

I go back to the garage with resentment dancing with my sadness.

The gasoline is in our store room. I started sprinkling it generously. On my instruments, my book, all the pages and the black stool.

My favorite guitar lies on the floor.

I soak them in gasoline and hatred.

The matchbox weighs in my hand as I strike the match.

What's the use to live here?

What's the use of saving this place?

What is the use to live anymore?

Tears blur my eyes as I look at the fire burning on the stick with clenched teeth.

I dropped the lit match.

The burn mark on my feet is a reminder. Of them. Of me. Of the bad and of the good.

I took many healing creams and a skin regeneration treatment to get rid of the burn but one way or another, the scar stayed. It was deep in my skin. It was a part of me.

I can't fucking remove it. I am stuck.

I step forward and into the garage and stood right in the middle of the room, exactly the same place where I took the suicidal attempt to burn myself.

I take a deep breath. A tear drops down my eyes as I close my eyes.

My weak heart beats as everything rushes back and hits me like a headache ball on a crane.

My stomach drops at the sudden intrusion of bad memories.

Suddenly I feel lightheaded and the black charred walls spin.

Chapter 39

CALLEN

"She's nice." Cam pats my back as I come back inside the house.

"Thank you for not hitting on her more than once."

"That's what brothers are for." He winks at me.

Mom and Dad are clearing dessert plates from the backyard. I help them.

"Didn't you drop her?"

"No, Dad. She has a meeting tomorrow."

"You could have asked her to stay over."

"I did. She insisted on going home and it's her first time in this house. Don't expect everything to happen within the first visit. Step by step is called a program."

"Fancy explanation for her not wanting to sleep with you tonight." Missy whispers teasingly as she passes by us.

I huff out in annoyance.

"Aria is a very beautiful girl. She is polite, funny and kind. She will be an amazing daughter in law." Mom says.

"I have no idea how you got her to like you but when miracles happen, we embrace them with no question." Dad throws his hand in the air.

"Thank you, Mom. And Dad? Please believe in me for once." I backpedal, waving them. "I need sleep. Good night."

We all had rooms in our parents' house even though Cam and I had our own apartments; our parents never tried changing our room.

I get out of the t-shirt and trousers, leaving them on the floor.

Aria would have scolded me for leaving a clothes trail.

Sorry, Angel. I am exhausted. I promise I will take it tomorrow.

I fall on my bed, face first.

I loved today. I loved having Aria beside me. I loved how perfectly she fits with my family.

God, today was perfect.

My eyes start drifting close. I don't know how long it has been since I fell asleep but a sound woke me up.

My phone is lit up and buzzed on the side table.

I turn the screen to see the caller ID.

Lexa.

Weird.

"Hello?" My voice comes out raspy.

What she says on the other line makes me sit upright.

"I am on my way." Is all I can say before disconnecting the call.

I quickly pick up the clothes off the ground to wear them with my heart beating so hard in my chest.

Aria is attached to tubes, needles and a heart rate machine.

The air was thick in the hospital room. Ver and Lexa sat on one side of the bed, holding Aria's hand tightly in theirs.

"What happened?" My voice comes out hoarse. It felt like someone was choking me.

"Her BP dropped, leading her to faint." Cam checks her vitals. He turns to me. "I thought you told she went back home."

"She did!" I say with a sudden outburst. "That's what she told me."

"I will come in an hour to check on her again. If she wakes up before that, call me."

Cam leaves the room. His eyes were tired and worried. I woke him up as soon as I got the call from Lexa. And he thankfully didn't make any scene of getting his beauty sleep and was equally tensed as me on the way here.

"Aria said that she had a meeting in the morning. That's why she insisted on leaving. Why was she in someone's house?"

Zeenat and Lexa exchange a hesitated look.

"Tell him. He deserves to know." Ver says tiredly. She puts her face down on the bed so she doesn't look at me.

Lexa starts talking. "Aria's parents separated when she was 15. But she didn't mind it much. Her parents mutually decided and for her what mattered the most was that her parents are happy. They had their own times, weekends over with their dad. They were happy."

"They were happy. Calliope, Astra and Ari." Zeenat continues, a faraway look comes on her face. "But one night when we were performing at a bar, they met with a car accident. Brakes fail. Astra was going to pick her mom up before they came back home. They *never* did."

"Her dad was the emergency contact and he called her and told everything. They went under surgery to save their lives but they didn't make it."

"Aria got so upset over it. She lost everything, you know. Her mom and sister were her world. She somehow felt if she didn't have them, nothing was worth living anymore." Her voice chokes up but she makes an effort to complete her sentence. "So she went back home and threw fuel over her garage and burnt it."

"Burnt it?" I gasp in shock. Why would Aria burn her garage?

She hesitates. "She was in the middle of the garage."

The air is knocked out of my lungs.

"She tried to burn herself?" I say it out loud to myself. It hurts even more saying than feeling. My angel, the bright spot in my life, tried to leave the world.

I bite my hand in my mouth from screaming. *Fuck.*

They don't say anything but it doesn't change this.

"Hey guys, we have a meeting in 20 minutes. We better get going." Ver notices the time.

"Callen, can you stay with her till we finish the meeting?"

"Of course. I'm not leaving her side." I sit beside Aria on the chair.

Ver and Lexa leave the room but Zeenat lingers back.

"Hey, Callen?"

"Yeah?"

"Aria is a good person."

"I never doubted that even for a second." I say without an ounce of hesitation.

"And even if she doesn't admit to herself, she has opened her heart to you."

I squeeze Aria's hand.

"She loves you, Callen."

"I love her too." Tears well up in my eyes.

"Please be there for her."

I nod because I don't trust my own voice.

"You both are perfect for each other." The door closes behind her.

I lay my head on Aria's stomach, letting the tears flow.

221

I ached for her. She suffered. She broke herself and somehow taped the piece back. All I want her to do right now is be healthy and live. I want her to smile with no shadows in her eyes. I want to love her and make her the happiest she has ever been.

"I love you, Aria." I whisper against the blanket.

Chapter 40

ARIA

I feel a weight on my stomach before my eyes open. My throat is parched and my eyes are swollen as I open them. Bright light burns into them. I lift a heavy hand to rub them.

Where am I?

The weight on my stomach is still not lifted. A black bush of hair is what I see immediately. I recognize it as Callen's. I could figure out him only by his smell and physique.

I pass a hand over his hair as I try to remember what happened.

I went to Callen's house. Met his family. That made me miss my family so after 4 years of not stepping into the house I grew up in, I finally went inside.

Callen lifts his head up, sleepy eyes snapped into attention when he saw me.

"Oh my god, Aria." He swoops me into his arm. My body aches after not moving for a long time. And my head hurts.

"Ow ow!" I bite down on my lip in pain.

"I'm sorry, I'm sorry. Are you okay?" He frees me from the hug.

"What happened?" I ask, massaging my hands and wiggling my toes. They are stiff.

"You fainted because your blood pressure dropped. What were you doing in that old house, Aria?"

"Wow, getting directly to the point, are we?" I joke, but Callen doesn't laugh; only concern shines in his eyes.

"Whatever I tell you, promise me you won't think of me like a freak."

"If you are a freak then I don't know what the rest of the world is called, sweetheart."

I smile a little.

"It was my parents' house. Mom's specifically."

I proceed on to tell him about Mom, Astra, Dad and the divorce. I told him about the night of the accident. I tell him everything.

"I have laid myself bare, Callen. This is me. Shattered pieces of a glass vase. Do you still find my jadedness beautiful?"

"I will spend my whole life piecing you back. It doesn't matter to me."

"Sharp edges of the glass can cut."

"I will bleed then. Only for you, my angel. Why did you go to your Mom's house?"

"Seeing your family made me miss mine. And I know they're dead and going to the cemetery would have been a better option. But I didn't want to surround myself with dead bodies so I went home. It had happy memories, not corpses."

"I am sorry, Aria."

"I am sorry too. I should have been honest with you."

"You told me now. That's all that matters." Callen weaves his hand through mine. "What about your dad?"

"I haven't spoken to him or seen him ever since the night after the accident."

"Oh, Aria."

"I know. It's not exactly good daughter behavior."

"We'll work on it, okay?"

"We?"

"You would be crazy to think that I am ever leaving you."

"But I have so much of emotional package." I gesture at myself. I am literally in a hospital bed, telling him the worst days of my life.

"So does everyone. I don't think anyone leads a happy life. Aria, look into my eyes. It hurts me when you are hurting. You are so important to me, baby. I am never letting you go, Angel."

He doesn't say anything more but kisses my forehead.

I close my eyes, soaking it all.

He sticks by me. He doesn't run for the hills when I show him my wild cards. He wants to stay.

My heart aches.

Why do I love you so much, Callen Cox?

Chapter 41

ARIA

"How's your health?"

"Good. I kept up with my doctor appointment."

"I worry about you, Bastian." Cash speaks through the phone.

"And I worry about you, Cash. Ver is going off like crazy."

"I know. But I really appreciate your help. After you took over the catering and decor, Ver is sleeping better. And she isn't so aggressive in sex so much."

"Do I count that as a good thing?" I ask laughing.

"My back is scratched raw."

"Don't tell me that. I don't want to know about my friend's sex life."

"But she tells you all about it, right?"

"Yeah, she does."

"Exactly. So just the mode of information freaks you out."

"C'mon. You are like a brother to me. I have known you since high school."

"I know Bastian and thank you for sticking with me." I honk the horn at the car in the front of me who driving too slow in the suburbs. "You're driving?"

"Uh huh."

"Where are you going?"

"If I tell you, will you promise me not to say anything to Ver?"

"Promise."

"Mom's house."

"Aria." He scolds.

"I know, I know. My blood pressure dropped last time I was there and I fainted in an abandoned house but this time, I have come prepared."

"Mentally and physically?"

"Well, I do have a cardboard box to clear up a few things."

"That answers a lot."

"Trust me on this, please. Listen, I am driving up to the curb. Call you later?"

"As soon as you leave the house, okay?"

"Love you."

"Love you too, Bastian."

I pull up to the curb of my house. Alone and lonely, just standing there. I take the box from the passenger seat and lock my car.

Last time, I fainted. This time, I am going to step out of that house with full consciousness and peace of mind.

I pass the porch, not looking at Mom's chair. Instead of going to the garage, I take the stairs. To our bedrooms upstairs.

I send people over to clean. They aren't allowed to touch or position anything differently.

I take the left, Mom's room, as soon as I climb up stairs.

After Dad left, I slept in Mom's room so many times but she never minded that we had our own rooms and still wanted to sleep in the same bed with her.

227

The floral pink bed sheet with fluffed up pillows. Her bed.

I opened the first drawer. Her dresses, her clothes washed and neatly folded. I closed it. I checked the remaining three drawers and they are exactly the way they left it but clean.

I moved to her dressing table.

In the second drawer, I see a glint of silver. I pick it up. Her wedding ring shines in my palm. I kept it in the cardboard box. The vase she loved so much is beside her bed. I keep that in the box too.

Don't overthink, move on.

Next stop, the attic.

Dust falls on my face when I pull the attic door open. I sneeze as the dust tickles my nose. Ladder to the attic unfolds down.

Holding the ladder on one side while balancing the box on my hip, I climb up.

We had a small circle window in the attic that illuminates light everywhere.

I rummage through the dusty box and labeled bags. I find photo albums, DVDs and mix tapes that Dad made for Mama. They're all still here.

I almost trip over a box as I am looking around. I check the name.

Christmas decorations in Mama's handwriting.

Christmas is coming soon. Maybe I should decorate Mama's ornaments on our Christmas tree this year.

There's a sharp pang on my chest.

I forgot that all these things even existed till I came looking. There have been 4 Christmases since they died and these ornaments aren't hung up since then.

Who knew that their last Christmas would be their last Christmas?

I look around the attic. The forgotten attic with memories tucked in every corner, every box.

I didn't want to forget Mama and Astra. But I have, haven't I?

I rarely visited. Their things have been left untouched. I don't mention them anymore. It's like they are fading away...

How the hell could I be so inconsiderate?

I pick up the ornaments box and another one I bought with myself and rush down the ladder.

I have an idea and I really hope it works.

I breeze past everyone. I can hear them saying 'good morning's and 'hello's but my mind is focused on one place.

The studio.

I burst in and took the girls by surprise.

"Where were you, Aria?" Ver asks. "We tried calling you so many times. We need to finalize the songs for the album."

If she doesn't know, it means that Cash didn't tell her. *Thank you, Cash.*

"I think I want to add one more song." I say in desperation.

"What? You know we can't do that." Hayes refuses. Not paying any heed to him, I sat on the seat, taking the headphones to my ears.

"Please, it's important." I am pleading now. I don't think I have ever pleaded in my life.

"Aria, we can't." Hayes shakes his head.

The girls understand the desperation in my voice.

"Why don't you back off a little, Hayes?" Lexa shoos him, taking a seat beside me. "What do you need, babe?"

"Yes, we will help you. Go ahead." Zeenat rubs my shoulder and Ver gives me a reassuring nod as she whips out her notebook.

Hayes huffs in annoyance, leaving the room.

I look around on the soundboard. What do I want?

I want to remember Mama.

I want to remember Astra.

I want to make them immortal.

And how do singers make their important people immortal?

Chapter 42

CALLEN

"Hey, guys." Cash Flow greets us as he takes a seat beside.

There is a moment of shock before we recover ourselves. Even though Cash is a natural occurrence now that I'm dating Aria, we always have a moment of shock. He's still our idol.

"Hey."

"Hi."

"What's up?" Erupt around the table.

"Are you excited for the girls' performance?" He asks.

"Hell yeah."

Aria texted me a while ago. According to her, the next performance is her band's and she has a surprise for us.

The host came up on the stage.

"Now, we have the greatest girl band singing their new single. Give it up for the Celestials!"

The thunders of claps are loud and excited.

The light dims, focusing on a piano. Aria walks onto the stage. Wearing a glittery black long dress.

She sits on the seat. Right in front of the piano.

She's going to play?

"Hi everyone. The song we're going to sing hasn't been released yet but there was no better time than now to sing this song to you." Aria says into the mic in front of her, smiling innocently. The light focus comes on Zeenat, Lexa and Ver. All standing in a row with mic stands in front of them, wearing the same pattern of dress that Aria is.

Aria starts playing the piano. The starting is beautiful.

"This is for my mom and my sister. I will always remember you."

The girls vocalize together.

I ran out
I didn't wait
The pain of losing you was too much to take
It's been a long time since I have come around
And I am sorry for not visiting you earlier

It's been a couple of difficult months
When you left, you left me alone
I took it on me to be the queen and soldier of this castle

But now it's time to make amends

First things first,
I want to say that I am sorry
For not being here earlier
I should have been there
But I had too much regret
I did not think straight

No time for goodbyes,
No time to tell you how much I loved you
If you only knew, I never wanted you to leave
And write in the sky that I will always remember you
Maybe then years won't erase you

The girls vocalize and Aria is playing the piano in full force. Her eyes shut but when she looks at her friends, she smiles and they vocalize together because pain and love binds them together.

Maybe we will meet one day again and I get to tell you
how much I loved you
Till that I will wait
I will live waiting for you
And I will write in every space
I love you in every place

The crowd claps with a standing ovation. I see so many people crying. I rise up to my feet, clapping proudly.

Aria leaves the piano to hug her band. They whisper something to each other with tears and smiles.

The hosts come again to the stage and their eyes are misty and they thank Celestials and announce the next performance.

"I will be back in a minute." I am out of my seat and rushing backstage.

I found Aria almost immediately. She's leaning on the railing, hands on each side of it. Head hanging down and shoulders shaking lightly.

"Ari?"

Her head snaps to my voice.

"Callen?" Her face is tear stricken but she looks calm, relieved and *happy*.

She leaps into my arms.

"Hi hi hi."

"Hey angel." I swipe a hand over her hair.

"Did you like the song?" She asks, smiling.

"I can't believe you wrote one for them."

"I had to. They are so special to me. They always will be. I have to remember them in a good way. They're my *family*."

I hugged her again. "I am so proud of you." I say into her hair.

"Callen?"

"Yes, Angel."

"I love you."

My heart skips a beat. "What?"

"I love you, Callen Cox. I fucking love you. And I've been in love with you ever since you chose *California Dreamin* to play in my car stereo. Thank you so much for being with me, tolerating me and never giving up on me, even when I'm difficult. Thank you for showing me that I am capable to love again, baby."

"I love you too. Maybe even more."

"Then we got a problem, buddy. Because last time I checked, I love you more." She pats my chest.

I laugh, kissing her. "I love you. *So damn much*."

She relaxes into me.

She's happy. She's not carrying the burden of her mom and sister anymore. She's at peace.

Her happiness makes me happy.

I have her and I love her.

She's mine and I'm hers.

EPILOGUE

"Callen, I don't think I can do this." I cry into the phone. This is scary and I just wanted to boink my head on the steering wheel.

"Angel, no one is happier than me of all the progress you have made. You are so strong." Callen encourages from the other side of the line. "You know I wouldn't have asked you something if I felt like you're not ready for it."

"Maybe I *am* not ready."

"Yes, you are. You are going to regret not inviting your dad to our wedding. I would have come with you but this first meeting is yours to do." The engagement ring shines in the sun.

I'm not scared to talk to my Dad. I am scared that he *won't* talk to me.

"What if he turns me away? I haven't exactly been the best daughter to him in the last few years."

"That's what second chances are for. You were a teen. You lost the most important people in your life. I don't know about others but I obviously don't expect you to act sane. Now that an opportunity has presented itself grab it before, it's too late."

"Okay."

"Calliope and Astra would be happy."

I bit my lip. "I know."

"I love you, my angel."

"I love you too, Cal."

"Call me after you're done, okay?"

"Okay."

I look out of the window. Dad's apartment is so monotone. I step out of my car, locking it.

Apartment 121. That's what the owner of the building told me. How easily he told me shocked me, I didn't even need to name drop to get the information. That's how bad the security of the building was. If Dad lets me help him out, I will shift him to a better, cleaner and safer house soon.

When we were making the invite list, Callen suggested that I invite Dad. I obviously cowered. What explanation would I give to Dad to cut him off completely? He just didn't lose his wife and elder daughter. He also lost his younger daughter due to ignorance.

He lost his family.

The elevator dings to the floor.

121 is right in front of me as the metallic doors open.

I stand outside the apartment, hands raised to ring the bell.

Maybe I should go. This is a bad idea.

The door suddenly opens and I am standing face to face with... Dad.

Years and years of not him. And there he was.

His familiar eyes widened in surprise at me and I don't think mine are any smaller than a saucer.

"D-dad?"

A disbelief gasp leaves his mouth.

"Aria." His tall, bulky figure engulfs me into his arm without a question. A garbage bag drops near our feet. Tears immediately wet my neck. "Oh dear."

I missed you, Dad.

I hugged him back hesitantly. It's been so long since I hugged him. He feels like childhood memories and comfort.

He detaches himself from me and turns his head, looking back into his apartment. "I am sorry. The apartment is a bit shabby."

"It doesn't matter, Dad."

"Hey, congratulations on your engagement. He seems like a good guy." Dad says well naturally but listening to him pains me.

He had to know about my engagement from the news, rather than me. And what makes the pain intensify is that he doesn't even sound or look resentful. He is genuinely happy for me.

He deserves so much better.

He deserves a better version of me.

"Hey Dad, can we talk?"

"Sure, come in."

I stepped into the apartment that was my Dad's but I never lived here before.

"Do you want coffee or tea?" He asks, closing the door, leaving the long forgotten trash bag on the threshold.

"Can I have cocoa?"

He smiles. It looks foreign on his face, straining against it. He didn't smile much, did he?

"Coming right up."

"Can we talk first? Before anything else."

He nods, sitting on the worn couch.

I sit on the opposite side.

"I know I don't deserve your forgiveness after all I have done to you. I have ignored you and abandoned you when you needed me the most. I'm sorry. Someone once told me that relationships are hard. They are difficult to understand and are pointless if you think about them. But one good thing that comes out of it is you learn how to love. You love and you learn. You learn what's important. And sometimes, you screw up. But that's what second chances are for. To learn from all things you did wrong and make it right again. So Dad, can I make all the wrongs I have done to you right again?"

"Of course, Aria Ryanne. *Of course*. But only if you promise me if I input into this too. Even I have done my own fair share to screw up."

"We got all the time in the world, Dad."

He reaches for her hand, enveloping in his big ones. "We do."

"Also, I forgot to give you this." I handed him the wedding invitation from my purse. He takes it, tears in his eyes. He opens it. He would see Callen and my name together with the only thing separating our name is *'wed'*.

Mr. and Mrs. Cox in making.

"I want you to walk me down the aisle."

Dad looks up from the wedding invitation. The tears were more prominent now. "You do?"

"There would be no one else other than you who I would love to walk me down the aisle."

"I would love to do it, Ryanne."

"We will also have two chairs in the front. For Mom and Astra."

He sniffles.

"I love you, Aria and I am so proud of you."

Seeing him cry makes me cry.

"Okay, let's go and make the cocoa?" I wipe away my tears.

"Sure."

Before joining Dad in the kitchen, I text Callen.

Aria- Spoke to Dad. He is happy to walk me down the aisle.

Callen- That's my girl.

Aria- Thank you for this, Cal. I wouldn't have done this if it wasn't for you.

Callen- This was all you, fiancée. God, I can't wait to call you my wife.

I smile at the phone.

6 years ago, I lost my world. I was feeling hopeless and desperate.

Now, I am rebuilding it again. Having all the people I love in it.

This is a good way to stay.

The End

Thanks for reading

If you enjoyed Sweet Melodies, please consider leaving a review on Amazon and Goodreads. Your support means the world to me and it will help other readers find my book.

Acknowledgements

I wrote my acknowledgements a month before my release but this whole month has been a rollercoaster so my thank yous deserved to be rewritten again.

First, my mom. Mama, you're amazing. You tolerate me when I'm annoying, you love me when I'm so unlovable and you stay with me in every step of life. I mean, you're my mother. Where else would you go? Hahaha, but still. You have always been there for me and I promise I will be there for you too. You're the world's best mom. I hope I can make you proud.

To my sister, Alina. Making me your sister showed me what love actually is. And even anger because you're really annoying. But what I have with you is something I could never trade. You're my little sister, my lifeline and my everything. I love you, Alina and I can't wait to see you grow up to be an amazing women.

To my dad. Papa, I have seen your dreams all my life. I have seen you want something and I have seen you work day and night for it. You are an epitome of hard work and you have shown me that dreams are not the ones you see in your sleep and day dream for your future, dreams are the one you chase after because if you love something so much, if you're passionate about it, you achieve it. There were so many times I wanted to give up as I wrote this book but seeing you made me realize that I shouldn't. This is my dream and I will chase it till it becomes a reality.

To my grandmother. Mimi, you are my role model. You have shown me what it's like to be a woman. You showed me I am strong and that I am worth something. I am always thankful for you and I promise to carry your legacy forward.

To my beta readers, Samyukta, Mohul, Maha and Lavanya. You girls are my first readers ever and fueled me when I couldn't find the fire in myself. I love you girls from the bottom of my heart and I hope we go a long way.

To my best friends, Lina 'tiny' Yasmine and Sadhika Shree, you both have somehow tolerated my ass for 10 years and we are counting more years together. Thank you for being attentive listeners to my venting sessions. For choosing posts which look good enough to post. And the undying support and sweet words. This book was possible because you were my anchors. Thank you my 4C gang.

To Ikhlas, you wouldn't believe that I wrote a book but you read the first, very rough draft and you fell harder for Aria and Callen than anyone else could. You claimed their moments and I am so happy about it. Igloo, you are amazing.

To Nina Bloom, my mentor. I couldn't have asked for a better friend and supporter than you. I can't wait to write more books by your side, become bestselling authors and do book signings together.

To my bookstagram friends, who loved and showed excitement over the book that was still under covers back then. You are the reason why I believed in this story and myself.

Last but definitely not the least in my eyes, who read the book. You. You made it this far and honestly, that is enough.

New series coming 2023

H.A.W (April/ May 2023)

About the author

Wafiyah Basha is a New Adult fiction author.

She has always had a knack for writing, ever since she was a kid. When she was 16, she had too many ideas to hold in her head, so she did what any rational person would do. Starting to make up fake scenarios of her characters falling in love with each other and overcoming all the obstacles.

Her debut novel was published in 2022, and she won't stop writing more heart-clenching, flawed, and lovable characters till the end of time.

She likes baking, cooking, reading, and obviously, writing, because you wouldn't be reading this if she hadn't taken the next step and published her novels.

Catch her active on Instagram, where she posts things that probably not everyone is interested in. But does that stop her? No, it doesn't. Thank you very much.

Printed in Great Britain
by Amazon